THE HARDER THEY FALL

"Tell me what I want to know or—" Slocum said.

"Or what?" the duchess said, her dark eyes catching the fire of anger now. "You will make me? With Mikhail standing there?"

"He's a big man," Slocum said. "I'd hate to hurt him."

"Hurt Mikhail? That is rich!" Her anger changed mercurially to humor. She laughed, but it was artificial.

"I remove him, Duchess," Mikhail said.

Reaching the end of his patience, Slocum half turned, feinted right, then swung with all his might and landed a left fist in the Russian's solar plexus.

For a moment, Mikhail stood stock-still. Then he let out a tiny woof and simply sat down. A few twitches showed that he was still alive but not up to fighting Slocum.

Slocum turned back to the duchess. "You were telling me about Scoggins."

JAKE LOGAN

SLOCUM AT DEVIL'S MOUTH

J

JOVE BOOKS, NEW YORK

SLOCUM AT DEVIL'S MOUTH

A Jove Book / published by arrangement with
the author

PRINTING HISTORY
Jove edition / March 2003

Copyright © 2003 by Penguin Putnam Inc.

For information address: The Berkley Publishing Group,
a division of Penguin Putnam Inc.,
375 Hudson Street, New York, New York 10014.

ISBN: 0-515-13492-9

A JOVE BOOK®
Jove Books are published by The Berkley Publishing Group,
a division of Penguin Putnam Inc.,
375 Hudson Street, New York, New York 10014.
JOVE and the "J" design
are trademarks belonging to Penguin Putnam Inc.

PRINTED IN THE UNITED STATES OF AMERICA

10 9 8 7 6 5 4 3 2 1

1

The frigid wind whined like a banshee gnawing at John Slocum's face. With a crunching sound that drowned out the strong gusts, he pulled his frozen, broad-brimmed hat down to protect himself a little more, but it did no good. The wind had an uncanny way of sneaking up and attacking the already raw flesh on his cheeks and lips hidden under his tattered blue bandanna. His nose had turned into a benumbed lump an hour earlier, and any chance of smelling anything on the wind had died along with the frostbite. His belly grumbled from lack of food, but Slocum knew better than to stop now for even a handful of parched corn from his meager hoard. He had made a bad decision to keep moving and beat the storm. Now he had to live—or die—with that choice. Tingling ran up and down his legs, and if he dismounted to hunt for any tidbit to eat, he might never get back into the saddle. As a new gust rocked him, he worried that he might have to tie himself in place.

Slocum knew when his eyes watered and the tears froze immediately, he had to find shelter. The rapidly dropping temperature hinted at a real humdinger of a blizzard on the way, and Slocum knew such storms in midwinter blowing out of Canada across Dakota's Black Hills meant death to the unwary.

Or those stupid enough to keep riding, as he had done most of the day.

Even without a blizzard dumping ten feet of snow on his head, he might not survive without a place to ride out the blow he fought so tenaciously now.

"Keep going," he said grimly, reaching out a gloved hand to pat his horse's neck. The animal shuddered as his icy fingers touched it. Slocum straightened and heard ice cracking free of his arms and shoulders. Blinking hard, he cleared his eyes enough to look around.

To the north, in the direction of Goldust, where he headed, the clouds had turned a fierce black, roiling and boiling and promising only wintry death for anyone foolish enough to ride into the teeth of the storm. He turned slowly. Skin stretched and broke open. Warm blood trickled down inside his sleeves and under his shirt, in spite of the protection from his heavy canvas duster. More flesh had frozen than he'd thought.

Slocum scanned the rugged terrain for any place offering refuge. It was too much to hope that he could find a fallen tree to furnish wood for a fire. Getting a blaze going in this wind would require the fires of hell itself; none of the lucifers in his shirt pocket would do the trick. Rugged cliffs rose in the distance, but Slocum knew he could never get to them in time to cower in their dubious shelter. The windswept snow stretching out in a blinding white blanket all around showed wind drift marks like desert sand.

"Burning," Slocum said to himself, laughing a little hysterically. His fingers had stopped tingling and now felt as if he had thrust them into a fire. His laughter died as he shook off the shock of being so cold. In some dim recess of his paralyzed brain he realized he was freezing to death. His horse might make it to the boomtown of

Goldust, or even to Deadwood a dozen miles farther, but he would be a rock-hard frozen statue riding in the saddle. They might have to wait until spring thaw to get him into a proper coffin.

The notion of being buried frozen to his saddle shook him out of his stupor. A little.

He saw the track of a big snow rabbit heading off down a steep ravine and started to follow it. With luck he might find how the rabbit survived such vile weather, even if he couldn't dig down and join the critter in its warm burrow. As he tugged on the reins, Slocum almost tumbled from the saddle. He grabbed the saddle horn and steadied himself against a new gust of wind.

Slocum knew he was weakening fast. Hunger was part of it, as was thirst. But freezing to death presented the greatest threat.

Not having any other direction to go, he rode along following the rapidly vanishing rabbit tracks. Wind whirled and whistled, stirring the fallen snow and erasing the deep prints. Then a snow pellet struck him in the face. The leading edge of the new storm would do more than blow old snow around. It would bury the countryside under a new white shroud.

A shroud that would cover him.

"No," Slocum grumbled. "No, no, no!" Anger at his fate warmed him and sent fire surging through his arteries. He weakly kicked his heels and kept his horse stumbling along. The rabbit tracks disappeared quickly as the wind gained new strength, bringing blinding, stinging snow with it.

Slocum looked around for the tracks and realized he had lost them. He craned his neck, hunting for any sanctuary. Other than a few low hills rounded by wind erosion, he saw nothing. Those hills afforded no safety for him. Nowhere did, but he refused to give up. Slocum kept riding, angling to his right so the wind tormented his left side. When his arm felt nigh on useless, he angled back so his right arm bore the brunt of the storm. He couldn't simply face the storm head-on anymore. Not with the way his face felt.

Slocum drifted as he rode, then snapped to full attention. For a moment he thought he had died because hot air blew across him in the middle of this frozen hell.

"Whoa," he said, tugging on his reins. Slocum looked around, turning until the hot breeze struck him fully in the face. He hardly believed his luck. Squinting into the snowstorm, he hunted for the fire that had to be blazing higher than the Palace Hotel in San Francisco to create such a blast furnace gust.

There was no denying the heat, but he saw no fire. He clucked his tongue and snapped his reins to head his horse directly into the hot wind. All around, the swirling Dakota blizzard tried to rob him of this small measure of heat—and it failed.

Slocum didn't understand what he had found. One low hill appeared to be broken open. The snow in front of the rocky gash had melted, turning the dirt to mud. Ice refused to cling anywhere around the opening, leaving the rocks glistening with bright dampness. When his horse reared and almost threw him, Slocum realized the animal wanted to go into the heat blazing forth from the bowels of the earth.

"Whoa, there," he said, calming the mare the best he could. Taking great care, not wanting to lose the horse in the fierce blizzard now blotting out the rest of the countryside with a white curtain of stinging snow, he climbed down. Clutching the reins fiercely, Slocum stumbled forward on frostbitten feet to the opening.

He had been in deserts without water and had hallucinated. He had seen mirages and believed distant riders were much closer because of heat shimmer. But that had been in West Texas and in the Sonoran Desert. That had been where heat was his enemy.

He welcomed the constant buffeting of hot air against his face. As the ice melted from his eyelashes and his thawing cheeks began to tingle, he realized the snow caking the front of his heavy brown canvas duster had melted into a puddle around his boots.

Slocum didn't have to tug hard at all to get his horse through the ragged opening into the protecting cave. While narrow, it was large enough to accommodate the eager horse. Blundering along on his frozen feet and venturing deeper into the dark interior, he felt the hot wind against his face every step of the way. Even without the heat boiling out, the cave would have saved his life by giving shelter from the raging snowstorm.

When he reached a point where the pitch black was too much for him, he sank down, back pressed against a cool rock wall. Slocum left his horse to its own devices and sagged weakly, trying not to cry out in pain as his muscles began to recover from the frostbite. He didn't understand at first why the incessant whining wind from the cave interior was so warm, then realized it wasn't warm at all. If he had felt the wind in the middle of a scorching Dakota summer, it would have felt cool.

To him, frostbitten as he was, anything above freezing was hotter than a smithy's forge. This constant earth breath fell somewhere between freezing and scorching, and that was good enough to save him.

Water beaded on his duster and then trickled in sluggish freshets to the floor of the cave. Slocum shucked off his stiff gloves and reached down to feel the pools of water caused by the snow melting off him. He was reassured by how his sense of touch had returned. Unseen a few feet away, his horse nickered uneasily. The mare was a little spooked by the intense darkness and the warm air gusting endlessly from deeper in the cave. Slocum was too exhausted to comfort the horse. His muscles refused to move and his head spun in wild, crazy circles.

He pulled his damp duster closer around his quaking shoulders and turned so the warm breeze, whether from heaven or hell didn't matter, blew across his storm-ravaged face. He slumped forward and in a few minutes fell asleep, the whine of anguished, tortured souls carrying on the wind to his ears and dreams.

The snoring of some giant creature woke Slocum. He came to with a start, his arms shoving back hard against the cave wall. For a frightening second, he thought he had gone blind, then remembered how he had found this cave and its sheltering darkness.

The snores came from the incessantly gasping cave. Slocum had no idea why the air rushed out like it did, but it was warmer than the frigid land outside, and it had saved him. In complete darkness, he stretched sore, tired muscles and winced as his shirt pulled free of the spots where his skin had cracked open from the frostbite and bled sluggishly. Slow, deep breaths matching those of the cave settled him and let him slowly check himself for damage.

Although the tips of his fingers and toes remained numb, nothing had been permanently damaged. But the emptiness in his stomach told him it had been far too long since he had eaten. He had come north from Scotts Bluff, thinking to beat any bad weather. Slocum was seldom wrong when it came to making such estimates of travel time and dangerous weather, but he had been this time. He hadn't reckoned on the storm lingering over the Black Hills after it had blown out of the badlands to the east. The new storm had been a fierce Canadian one from the north and would have ended his trail if it hadn't been for this cave.

Luck had been with him, in spite of his poor judgment.

He got his feet under him and stood, braced against the wall for support.

He cocked his head to one side to block out the unrelenting wind blowing from the depths of the cave and heard his horse whinnying. Slocum turned in that direction and, using the wall as a guide, retraced his steps to the cave mouth.

The sudden brightness as he rounded a bend he had not remembered taking showed a land blanketed in dazzling white snow. It also showed something else he had not anticipated.

"What're you doing?" Slocum snapped. His voice came out rasping like a rusty hinge, but the words were enough to cause the thief rifling through Slocum's saddlebags to spin around. The man's face was hidden in shadow, and the bright outer light limned his body. He was tall and stoop-shouldered, showing bare, spindly arms as he reached over Slocum's saddle.

When Slocum didn't get an answer, he went for his Colt Navy slung in its cross-draw holster. He had forgotten he still wore his duster, and his hand slid across damp canvas. Fumbling, he pushed aside the heavy coat and grabbed for the ebony butt of his six-shooter. By the time he hauled it out, the thief had turned and bolted from the cave.

"Stop!" Slocum started to fire, but his thumb proved too numb to pull back the hammer. He took the six-gun in both hands and lifted it, but his chance had gone—and so had the man searching through his belongings.

Slocum ran past the skittish horse and came to a halt, his toes in the snow drifting up around the cave mouth. The storm had been so furious that it had dumped snow faster than the relentless wind could melt. But the sky was brilliant blue now, dotted with fleecy clouds, and the sun shone blindingly on the white carpet of snow.

It took Slocum only a second to find the man's tracks.

Amazingly, the man had arrived on foot and had left the same way. Slocum hardly believed anyone could survive the harsh weather without a horse. That might be why the man was so interested in Slocum's possessions. He was a horse thief and wanted to make off with a tired, frightened horse.

But that didn't make much sense. The man had been going through Slocum's saddlebags. He could have grabbed the reins and led the horse out, quickly vanishing into this wonderland of ice, snow and sparkling rainbow points.

Slocum started to mount and go after the crook, then stopped. His horse might not be up to the chase. For all that, Slocum wasn't sure he was, but he wanted to find out what the man had intended. If he was a simple sneak thief, he could be dispatched quickly enough. But he might have been stranded like Slocum and was nothing more than a pilgrim in need of help, crazed by his ordeal.

Slocum slid his six-shooter back into its holster and stepped out into the sunlight. The storm winds had died. Only the cool gusts at his back remained a constant in the deadly, lovely landscape. He stepped away from the cave and found himself in utter stillness. For a moment, he considered letting the man go. Then he knew he couldn't do that.

Whether the man was a robber or in trouble, Slocum had to find him and settle accounts. A bullet handled the first. Possibly the two of them could work together to reach Goldust if it were the latter.

Slocum plodded along, following the man's long stride through the snowdrifts. When he reached a rise looking down into a hollow, he caught sight of the man struggling along in the knee-deep snow.

"Stop!" Slocum shouted. His words rolled like a gunshot across the level area. The fleeing man jerked around, caught sight of Slocum, spun back and floundered through the snow at an even faster clip.

Slocum lit out after him. Using the man's imprints in the snow helped Slocum narrow the distance, but he noticed the man's stride was longer than his own. Since Slocum stood a full six feet tall, that made the man even taller and certainly ganglier. Grunting with the exertion even as he reveled in the feel of muscles responding more smoothly now after being frozen stiff, Slocum soon reached the spot where the man had sighted him in pursuit.

"Where'd you go?" Slocum shouted, expecting some response. It might have been a bullet or a shout, but he thought he could elicit some reaction. The man had vanished—but Slocum heard a familiar whining sound.

Advancing cautiously, he rounded a snowy dome and saw the telltale fan of melted snow in front of another asthmatically gasping cave mouth. Slocum stepped into the wind rushing from the earth and let it warm him after his hike through the snow. In the mud around the mouth he saw large boot prints. Fresh ones left by his quarry.

"Come on out. I don't mean you any harm, if you weren't trying to rob me." Slocum didn't expect any answer, and he didn't get one. But he also didn't hear any sound, other than the endless draft from the cave.

Pushing aside his duster, he drew his Colt and stepped up to the craggy entrance. This cave was somewhat larger than the one where he had sought refuge against the snowstorm. Somehow, the larger opening released less air. Slocum listened hard for any sound of the man he chased but heard nothing. He sniffed, thinking he might scent a cooking fire or animal mustiness. Like the cave he had used, this one seemed dead.

Inching forward, Slocum remained alert for a trap. He hadn't survived a killer storm to be bashed on the head by a scrawny scarecrow of a sneak thief. He rounded a

bend and found the familiar inky blackness ahead. Slocum
considered letting the matter lie, then found a new determination. Putting his six-gun down on a rocky ledge
where it would be near at hand, he groped about for his
tin of lucifers. He pulled them out, took one and struck
it. The flare dazzled him, then he held it in his left hand
while he grabbed for his pistol with his right.

The light cast dancing shadows from rocks lining the
way deeper into the cave. His quick green eyes caught
sight of footprints going straight into the depths. Other
scuff marks showed that the man had come and gone several times earlier. Slocum might have found the lair, or at
least a convenient hideout, for the sneak thief.

Stepping forward quickly now as the lucifer burned
down the dry wood shaft, Slocum looked around for any
sign the man was hiding amid the piles of rocks. He
started to call out when he heard sounds outside the cave.
Cursing his stupidity, he realized the man had lured him
into the cave, gotten out through some small vent hole
and had circled behind him. Slocum was the one trapped
in the cave now.

He dropped the lucifer. With a sulfurous hiss, it sizzled
out in the shallow water pooled on the cave floor. Slocum
let his eyes adapt a little to the light slashing through from
the cave mouth, then retreated. His finger twitched on the
trigger and then came back in a quick jerk. Slocum knew
better than to shoot like that, but he was on edge and his
hands hadn't returned to normal. The jerk on the trigger
came as much from surprise as it did from lack of muscle
control.

His shot ricocheted off the cave wall and sailed out into
the Dakota morning. The two men waiting outside with
leveled rifles were caught off guard and returned fire
wildly. Slocum's second shot caught one man on the upper arm, spinning him around. The other would-be backshooter levered in a new round and triggered it in

Slocum's direction. The bullet tore past Slocum's head, forcing him into a crouch.

Slocum was more in control now. He hadn't expected to find two gunmen behind him, obviously waiting to dry-gulch him. He fired again, squeezing the trigger in his usual deadly accurate fashion and was rewarded with an-other grunt. He had winged the same man as before with this shot.

The men realized they stood outlined by the radiant light off the snow and split, going to either side of the cave opening. Slocum cursed when he saw how quickly they regained their wits. He was trapped inside now. He could follow the man he had chased, assuming he wasn't one of the backshooters, or he could try to break free of the trap.

Thinking about it a moment, Slocum doubted the scrawny man he had followed after going through his sad-dlebags was outside. Both of the riflemen were shorter and stockier. He remained in a crouch, waiting for them to foolishly outline their heads against the white snow or the bright azure sky.

After several minutes, Slocum decided to take matters into his own hands. He had incredible patience learned while he was a sniper for the CSA during the war. More than once he had outwaited more impetuous enemies, but now he let his curiosity get the better of him. The two gunmen might have mistaken him for the gaunt thief. Af-ter all, Slocum hadn't been in Dakota Territory long enough to rile up anyone enough so they'd shoot him in the back.

Duckwalking until he was only a yard inside the mouth of the cave, Slocum took a deep breath, turned so the gusty wind from the cave was directly at his back and then exploded outward, ready for a gunfight.

He swung left and right and then back hunting for the

two men. The footprints and a trail of steaming blood droplets showed the direction they had fled.

But this was the only evidence Slocum had that he wasn't alone in the middle of the Black Hills.

2

John Slocum wasn't sure what to do. He turned back to let the cool air gusting from the cave wrap him in its airy embrace, then looked back across the snow-covered land, his eyes fixed on the boot prints of the two fleeing ambushers. The gangly man who had rifled through his saddlebags was probably hidden deeper in the cave, but he had not shot at Slocum. The two riflemen had. Slocum took a step after the backshooters, then stopped.

He put his Colt Navy back into its holster and thought hard on what had happened. Almost freezing to death in the storm had been bad luck, then finding the cave with its warm breath had saved him. After that his luck had turned bad again. One thief, two would-be murderers. It struck him as odd that such desolate terrain would be populated with so many outlaws, but they didn't call this area the badlands for nothing.

Laughing ruefully, he pulled his hat down a little to shade his eyes from the intense glare of the blinding Dakota sun reflecting off miles of freshly fallen snow and retraced his steps to the cave where he had weathered the storm. His horse had crept out and tentatively nibbled at hardy plants growing near the muddy opening.

Slocum checked his belongings but found nothing missing. He didn't have much to steal, and what he did have was old and battered. Reaching up, he touched his shirt pocket where the letter from his old buddy Matt Scoggins was securely tucked. Scoggins had written to Slocum in Denver and had hinted at fabulous wealth to be gained in Goldust. Hearing of the boomtown and the gold strikes nearby, Slocum had decided to join Scoggins, knowing the risks. If he partnered with Scoggins, he might get rich. And if there wasn't any hope of staking a decent claim, Slocum intended to move on.

Scoggins understood the way Slocum thought since he and Slocum shared much in the way they viewed the world.

"Enough of that," Slocum said to his mare, gently pulling her away from what remained of the apparently tasty rubber rabbitbrush. The horse had cropped it level with the ground and wanted more. It provided poor forage but better than nothing at all. When they reached Goldust, Slocum would see that the dependable horse got a bag of oats.

His belly grumbled, reminding him he had to put on a feed bag of his own soon or he might pass out from hunger. He had misjudged how good the hunting would be along the trail to Goldust and had lost some of his provisions fording a deep, cold stream down south a few days earlier.

Slocum swung into the saddle and let the mare accommodate herself to his weight. He started slowly, letting the horse pick her way through the snowbanks. Keeping a sharp eye out for the other three owlhoots he knew were in the area, he slowly wended his way north, then found a road marked with "Goldust" signs every hundred feet. Slocum was dog tired and hungry and it was a little before sundown. He was ready to call it a day.

The road was still icy and mud patches showed where

wagons had traveled it recently. But it was the smell that reached Slocum's nose before he spotted the boomtown that told him he was near civilization. Garbage and raw sewage and even a hint of burned wood wafted over the hill, guiding him as surely as any beacon. He topped a rise and looked down at Goldust.

Slocum had seen dozens of towns spring up when gold or silver was discovered. Virtually overnight they grew from a handful to hundreds or even thousands of eager prospectors and miners. Goldust was caught up in this frantic growth. There was no rhyme or reason to the way the streets had been laid out or new buildings constructed. The sound of carpenters working into the night mingled with the rattle of wagons and the raucous cries of miners finishing their work and coming to town to get drunk and whore.

Amid all the commotion Slocum heard a church bell ringing. He didn't pay much attention to the day of the week, but this might well be Sunday.

"There's one place not to look for Scoggins," he told his horse. His friend was more likely in a cathouse than a house of worship. Slocum walked his horse down what passed for a main street. The only reason he thought this was the improbably high number of saloons. He lost count at twenty, some of them sporting numbers rather than names because they had been built so fast.

Slocum knew they would disappear just as fast when the gold petered out. Until then, there were fortunes to be made.

Scoggins hadn't written how to find him. In a town of a few hundred, that wouldn't have been a problem, but Slocum reckoned that since Scoggins had sent the letter, Goldust had more than doubled in size. There might be a thousand or more prospectors in town now, all hungering to get rich.

One saloon caught Slocum's eye. His horse complained

at not being taken care of first, but Slocum ignored the mare. She had eaten some of the rabbitbrush. He left the horse tied near a water trough. He used the butt of his six-shooter to knock a hole in the thin ice so the horse could drink her fill.

Then he went into the Southern Belle Dance Hall and Gaming Parlor to drink his.

The instant he stepped inside, Slocum knew this was the kind of place Scoggins would frequent. The name alone told him his old partner would be drawn here. Scoggins fancied himself a ladies' man, especially with southern belles. Slocum had seen firsthand that this was true during wild nights in New Orleans's brothels and almost a month spent on riverboats paddlewheeling their way up and down the Mississippi.

The smoke hung like a thick curtain, but Slocum sucked it in and relished the flavor on his tongue. It had been since Denver that he'd had the fixings for a cigarette. He pushed his way through to the bar and waited for the barkeep to notice him. A dozen green felt–topped tables showed where the tinhorn gamblers plied their trade, and ladies of the evening came and went up the stairs to the cribs on the second floor. But nowhere in the crush did Slocum spot Matt Scoggins.

"Beer," Slocum said. He preferred whiskey but needed food to dull its edge. Getting drunk fifteen minutes after riding into town wasn't too smart.

The barkeep grunted, then drew a mug with a foamy head and shoved it in Slocum's direction.

"Fifty cents," he said.

"Mighty expensive beer."

"Mighty big crowd of thirsty miners," the barkeep shot back.

Slocum knew the reality of boomtowns and paid, then asked after Scoggins.

"Never heard of him, but then I only been in town a

week. Hell, this here place only went up two weeks back,"
the barkeep said. Then the man hurried off to sell a fifty-
dollar bottle of brandy to a gent claiming to have struck
it rich.

Slocum sipped at the beer and even got a little tipsy,
again warning him how little there was in his belly. He
kept an eye peeled for Scoggins but didn't spot the man.
After finishing his beer, Slocum wandered through the
saloon inquiring after his friend. No one knew or admitted
to knowing a Matt Scoggins.

Somewhat disheartened that he hadn't found Scoggins
in what seemed a likely spot, Slocum went out, grabbed
up the reins and led his horse toward a livery. He stopped
and stared when he saw a dozen horses tied to a rope
strung outside the barn. Peering in, he saw all the stalls
were filled, some of them with horses and their owners
sleeping on the straw below.

"You got business here, mister? Other than gawkin'?"

Slocum looked back to see a man holding a pitchfork.

"I need a place for my horse. Some grain and—"

"Ain't gonna be here. Got more customers than I got
fodder." The man pointed with his pitchfork. "And you
ain't gonna get no place to sleep here, neither. A spot in
a stall goes for twenty bucks a night. Gold. None of that
worthless scrip you newcomers try to pass off as money."

Riding in Slocum's pocket was a wad of greenbacks as
well as a few hundred dollars scrip issued on a Denver
bank. He wished now he had swallowed the loss of con-
verting it to silver and gold coin.

"If you're full up, where else in town might have a spot
for a traveler like me?"

"Don't know," the man said, spitting into a dirty snowbank. "Don't much care." With that, he pushed past Slocum, untied the first horse in the remuda and led it around
back where a small pile of hay had been pitched. The
horse avidly ate of the sparse fodder. It was all Slocum

could do to keep his mare from tugging free and joining her equine companion.

The only thing worse than a boomtown and its prices was a boomtown in the middle of winter. Slocum knew the real fortunes wouldn't be made in the mines but in the town, selling whiskey and supplies. And sleeping space in horse stalls.

That knowledge did nothing to feed his horse or find him a place to sleep. He walked the town's meandering streets, asking after Scoggins and looking for a café. The tiny restaurant he found provided his first good meal since leaving Denver. But no one in Goldust had heard of Matt Scoggins.

"You have any place for a man to spend the night?" Slocum asked the owner of the café.

"Not here, nowhere in this town, mister," the man said. "Me and my wife's got our whole danged family in a one-room shack. Eight of us, including my good-for-nothing brother-in-law."

"Know of anywhere else? I'd be willing to trade some work for sleeping space and some fodder for my horse."

"You're out of luck," the café owner said. "No amount of money'll buy those commodities. Not right now. Come spring, who knows. But now the town's overflowing with a hundred miners a day arriving to try their luck in the gold fields."

"Any big strikes?" Slocum asked.

"A few. Not many, but the ones who did find color have hit it big."

Slocum knew stories of a claim's production grew every time they were repeated, but that didn't affect him as much as lacking shelter for himself and his horse.

"Much obliged."

"Mister," the man said. "I don't know if it's so, but I heard tell there are a few line shacks abandoned along Polecat Ridge. A dozen claims were filed there and not a one turned up so much as fool's gold. The big strikes are all to the west, not the east."

"Thanks. I suppose it won't hurt to look for something along Polecat Ridge."

Slocum shivered when he stepped out into the early nighttime wind. When the sun dipped low on the horizon, it got powerful cold. By the time the sun set, it turned freezing again. This time he wasn't likely to find one of the curious caves with the cool air blowing out all night long.

He made his way back to the main street and looked around a dozen saloons for any sign of Scoggins. Inquiries to both the drunk and the sober failed to produce any hint of recognition at the name or description. Slocum was ready to give up and ride east for Polecat Ridge to see if he might find one of those abandoned shacks when he noticed a woman staring at him from across the main room of the Woebegone Soul Saloon.

He wasn't in the mood for a tumble in the hay, in spite of her being so pretty. But something in the way she stared at him hinted that she wasn't a Cyprian working in the saloon.

Slocum ordered a whiskey to keep him warm, downed it in a gulp and started away when he felt a tentative touch at his arm.

"Wait, don't go," came the woman's plaintive request.

"Not interested," Slocum said, though he would have been under other circumstances. The woman's brown hair was mussed, and she had smudges of dirt that looked out of place on her pale oval face. Her clothing wasn't expensive, but it had been well mended and taken care of. Slocum pegged her as a woman of some means down on her luck.

"I'm not offering to sell myself," she said, recoiling.

"What are you doing in a dance hall then?" Slocum asked. Only fallen women frequented such places, though he had to admit the brunette woman seemed out of place here.

"I . . . I'm looking for my husband. My name's Elizabeth Bartlett. He's Ned Bartlett. He's a bit shorter than you and—"

"I just blew into town," Slocum said, cutting off her sorry story. "I'm looking for my own partner and not having any luck."

"Maybe if I help you find him, you can help me find my Ned!"

"You know a miner named Matt Scoggins?"

"I, uh, no, I don't. But I can help you look. We can look together." Elizabeth sounded frantic now, a touch of hysteria entering her voice.

"It's getting cold outside," Slocum said. "Why don't you go crawl into your bed and start over in the morning?"

Tears welled in Elizabeth's mud-brown eyes. "I don't have anyplace to stay. Th-there's no place at all in this horrid town!"

Her plight plucked at Slocum's heartstrings, possibly because he was in the same fix.

"You have any belongings other than what's on your back?" he asked.

"I, well, yes. I hid my trunk outside town where no one'd find it."

"Trunk?"

"I came to town on the stagecoach this morning," she said. "The stage from Laramie. We were four days on the road, snowed in the last night at a way station outside town. I've been following Ned, trying to find him for so long."

Slocum didn't want to hear about her misadventures. He damned himself but said, "I've been told of a shack up on a nearby ridge where we might spend the night. Not likely to be too fancy but walls and a roof would go a long way toward keeping us from freezing."

"I'll do anything, mister," she said.

"Slocum, John Slocum."

"Thank you, Mr. Slocum. You're the first one in Goldust who has shown me any kindness at all."

"It's mighty hard for a woman who has no intention of working in a saloon to find a job," Slocum allowed. In Goldust it might be well on impossible.

They stepped out into the increasingly bitter wind. Slocum fetched his horse and walked alongside it with Elizabeth Bartlett hurrying to match his long-legged pace.

"I don't have a horse," the brunette rambled on, filling the void when it was obvious Slocum wasn't going to do much talking. "Is it possible for me to take my trunk? I mean, all I own is in it and—"

"Take out what you can use tonight," Slocum said, seeing the large trunk half hidden by a green ash tree. "Leave the rest and you can get it tomorrow."

"I won't take much," Elizabeth said, pawing through the trunk. She took out items and put them into piles, then replaced them until Slocum wanted to do the choosing for her. She finally made up her mind and clutched the thick clothing to her bosom.

"You ride," Slocum said. "I can walk for a spell."

"Oh, no, it's your horse, Mr. Slocum. I can—"

"Keep a lookout for a line shack," Slocum said, peering through the gloom at a sign pointing the direction to Polecat Ridge. He trudged up the road, hardly listening to Elizabeth rattle on and on about her hunt for her husband. From what Slocum could tell, the man had left her in Salt Lake City. The reasons weren't too clear, but Elizabeth probably didn't know them. If Ned Bartlett had grown as tired of the woman's constant yammering as he had in a few short minutes, Slocum understood why the man had lit out to find his fortune somewhere else, somewhere far away from Mrs. Bartlett.

"There, Mr. Slocum. A tumbledown structure."

Slocum had already spotted the line shack and headed for it. He called out to see if anyone might be inside. Getting no answer, he rapped sharply on the door, knocking it into the small shack.

"Reckon the owner's either mighty poor at repairs or this place is abandoned." Slocum poked his head inside, then lit a lucifer and looked around. Nothing remained but crude wood furniture, a table and a narrow bed. Where a stove had been a hole gaped in the wall. The previous owner had taken both the stove and stovepipe when he had moved on.

"We have ourselves a place to stay then," Elizabeth said more cheerfully than before. She agilely dismounted and went inside, humming to herself. "The bed is a mite small."

"All yours," Slocum said. "I can pitch my bedroll on the floor."

"It'll be mighty cold on a dirt floor," she said. Something about the way she spoke put Slocum on edge.

"I'll be all right. Let me see if there's some firewood around. We can built a fire in a pit near the hole in the wall."

"I'll arrange things," Elizabeth said. Again there was something in the way she spoke that made Slocum wary. He found a woodpile out back and a dozen logs that would keep them warm through the night. Returning, he saw that Elizabeth had already scraped a small pit in the hard floor and had laid out their bedding.

Side by side.

Slocum wasn't going to argue with that. Heat was a scarce commodity as he had found out the night before.

Still . . .

"There, we have a fire," she said, after helping Slocum get it going. "We don't want too large a one or the shack will fill with smoke."

"I wouldn't worry about that," Slocum said, seeing cracks large enough to shove his fingers through between the planks making up the walls. He didn't doubt the roof was similarly leaky.

But the walls broke the worst of the bitter wind. That was all he had hoped for, that and to give his horse a leeward berth for the night.

Slocum stretched out and pulled his blankets up around his shoulders. It didn't surprise him too much when Elizabeth lay beside him, then scooted closer until she could half turn and wrap arms and warm legs around him.

Her hot breath gusted in his ear, a marked difference from the frostbite he had suffered the night before.

"Help me, John, and I'll help you. Help me find my husband, and I'll do more than keep you warm all night long."

He felt her arm snake around his body and move across his chest. Dancing fingers worked lower and came to his crotch to squeeze gently. Slocum started to respond.

Then he grabbed the woman's slender wrist and pulled it away. He didn't know if he was a fool or a damned fool for turning her down. But that's what he did.

"Sleep," he said gruffly. "Nothing else."

"But, John, I—"

He turned in such a way that the blanket fell like a curtain between them. Slocum faced away, staring at the small fire and wondering why he was passing up what the woman so freely offered.

No answer came as he drifted off to a troubled sleep filled with snowstorms and gasping giants buried in the earth.

3

The whistle of wind died just before sunrise. Slocum stirred, disengaged from the blanket wrapping him like shroud around a corpse in a coffin and sat up. Elizabeth Bartlett lay beside him on the dirt floor, her lovely face almost hidden in the tangle of blankets. He tried to figure why he had turned down her advances the night before. It might have been that she was married, but Slocum didn't think so—not entirely, though it bothered him how a married woman would want him when she was hunting for her husband. She was about the prettiest filly he had seen in months and months, and there was no denying she was willing, too.

They could have spent the cold, dreary night in a powerful lot of passion. But Slocum just didn't feel right about her and couldn't say why.

He pushed back the blankets and stood, shivering in the cold. He pulled on his boots and buckled his gun belt around his waist, then settled his duster around him. The canvas was stiff and took a few minutes to loosen up after he put it on. When his body heat was adequate, he went to the door and peered out along Polecat Ridge.

Tiny footprints in the crusty snow showed how the

name had come about. He made out tracks from several
skunks frolicking in the snowbanks, chased off by a larger
predator willing to endure stench in return for a decent
meal. Slocum felt the same way. His belly was grumbling
again, in spite of having had a large meal in the Goldust
café the day before.

He slipped past the rickety door and went to tend his
horse. It took the better part of an hour to dig down
through the snow to find enough sage and rubber rabbitbrush for the mare, but the animal ate gratefully when he
piled it up. Slocum wished his own hunger could be as
easily assuaged.

He touched the lump made by his six-shooter under his
duster, and considered his chances of bagging a snow rabbit. They didn't look good even when he hiked a hundred
yards away from the shack and the possible warning
scents left there by its former inhabitant. His sharp eyes
didn't miss a single track in the snow, and nothing worth
eating had come this way since the last snowfall. Disgusted with his poor luck, he returned to the shack to find
Elizabeth stirring.

Slocum caught his breath as she reached high above
her head, stretching like a sinuous cat. Her breasts flat-
tened a little, then came back full and round and firm
under her blouse. The woman's skirts were hiked up to
reveal more than her ankles. He saw bare calves and even
got a hint of fleshy thigh.

She noticed him and smiled just a little, in obvious
invitation because she made no move to cover herself.

"Where have you been, John?" she asked.

"Looking for breakfast. Polecat Ridge is too well
named," he said. "There's nothing worth bagging here."

"From the look of the tailings, there's no gold, either,"
Elizabeth said.

"You know about such things?" Slocum asked. Her offhand remark didn't surprise him that much. There was

more mystery about the brunette woman than there was knowledge.

"I know about a lot of things," she said, again moving her skirt up so he caught sight of tantalizingly naked flesh. But the cold forced her to give up on her attempts at seduction when he didn't immediately respond to her overtures. Elizabeth got to her feet, pulled the blanket around her quaking shoulders and heaved a deep sigh. "No food?"

"No food," he agreed. "We ought to be glad for the shack."

"I need to find my husband," she said, an edge in her voice that hadn't been there before. He wondered what Elizabeth would do when she found him.

They made their way down the muddy, half-frozen road back to Goldust. Slocum was amazed at the steady inflow of new prospectors, coming on foot and by mule and on the morning stage. The poor roads and isolation of Goldust didn't deter any of them or their optimism about striking it rich. A few hardly paused in town before heading out to grab their ounce of gold and glory, but many lingered.

"Go on, John," Elizabeth told him. "You're hunting for your friend, and I'm looking for my husband. If you hear anything about him, you'll let me know?"

"Of course," he said. "Where can I find you?"

Elizabeth shrugged and said simply, "Around." With that she headed into the maze of streets and vanished quickly without so much as a backward glance. Slocum considered himself well rid of her, in spite of her good looks and obliging ways. He unfastened the front of his duster, reached inside and made certain his six-shooter was riding easy, then went into the first saloon to begin asking after Matt Scoggins.

After an entire day of moving from one gin mill to the next, Slocum was tired of foot and soul when he decided to get a drink and find a place to bed down for the night. He wasn't sure he wanted to go back up onto Polecat Ridge, with or without Elizabeth Bartlett, but the shack was better than remaining out in the cold in town. Crime ran rampant, and the residents had apparently not bothered to hire a marshal. That would come later, if Goldust survived long enough.

"Whiskey," he said to the barkeep of the tent saloon where he had decided to end his daylong hunt. Dusk crept along the muddy, freezing streets and warned that it would be dangerous being exposed in another hour or two.

"Ain't got none. Brandy?"

Slocum looked dubiously at the bottle. Brandy all too often was nothing more than grain alcohol with nitric acid and some peach pits tossed in for flavor. He was past caring. He hadn't found Scoggins or anyone who even claimed to have seen him and was seriously considering traveling on. For that he needed some Dutch courage.

"A shot," he ordered. The barkeep poured the poisonous liquor into a foul glass. Slocum sipped at it, then knocked it back and put it down before the dizziness hit him. The brandy had the kick of a mule and turned his stomach inside out before tying it into a giant knot.

"Whew," he said, gasping.

"Good stuff, ain't it?" the bartender said, grinning ear to ear. "I make it myself." He moved on to let Slocum catch his breath before trying to sell another shot.

Slocum turned, then stared at a man coming into the tent. At first he didn't place him, then the man reached out clumsily to hold open the tent flap. He had been shot in the arm and shoulder, from the look of his bandages. At the same time Slocum reacted, the man looked up and locked eyes.

"Stop!" Slocum shouted, but the man lit out like a scalded dog. Slocum tore past a pair of drunken miners and burst into the night-cloaked street after the man. Slo-

cum was sure this was one of the pair who had tried to
gun him down on his way into Goldust.

For a moment Slocum lost his quarry, then saw him
separate from a crowd of miners and dart down an ad-
joining street. Slocum wasted no time going after him. He
had a score to settle—and some questions to get answered. While the owlhoot might have been out to rob
anyone he and his partner found, Slocum had the gut feeling their attack on him amounted to more than that. He
wanted to find out why they had been so eager to ventilate
him. If he couldn't locate Scoggins, then he would tend
to other business.

Bringing the backshooter to justice would relieve some
of the frustration he felt about Scoggins, about Elizabeth,
about even venturing northward into the Dakota Badlands.
He could have ridden south into Texas and spent a decent
winter along the Rio Grande, sampling tequila and the
señoritas there.

Slocum rounded the corner of the building. This street
snaked around sinuously, making it hard for him to spot
the running man. But he caught a glimpse as the outlaw
ducked into another saloon, thinking to lose him. Slocum's long stride covered the distance quickly. He pushed
through the swinging doors and crashed into a mountain.
Slocum recoiled, stumbled backward and then caught
himself against the doors. He had collided with a darkly
foreboding, bearded man dressed in well-kept furs who
towered above him.

"Sorry," Slocum said, trying to dodge around.

"You apologize," the man said, reaching out a hand the
size of a quart jar to grab Slocum by the shoulder. He
squeezed just a little and Slocum grunted in pain.

"I said I was sorry." He stepped back and sized up the
man. In addition to the fancy fur coat, he wore a black
hat with earflaps unlike anything Slocum had ever seen
before. Around the waist, the man had a broad leather belt

with heavy rifle cartridges held in leather loops, enough ammo to hunt a sizable herd of buffalo to extinction.

"I did not hear you. It is I who should then apologize."

The giant of a man seemed cheerful enough and not in the least impressed by the way Slocum had pulled back his duster so he could go for his Colt Navy. If anything, the man was oblivious to the lightning he almost unleashed by calling out Slocum.

Slocum stepped to one side and looked into the saloon. The sparse crowd couldn't have hidden the rifleman he was chasing. A partially opened back door told the story. Slocum's quarry had come in, passed through and left by the back way at a dead run. By now, he could be halfway to Deadwood.

"No offense taken," Slocum said glumly.

"I buy you a drink."

Slocum started to decline, then saw it might not be politic to do so. He had no quarrel with this huge man, and he had lost the owlhoot who had taken a potshot at him on his way to Goldust.

"And I will gratefully accept," Slocum said.

The colossus grinned, showing a bright gold tooth in front. He thrust out a monster of a hand that engulfed Slocum's. For a moment, there was a test of wills, each trying to apply more punishing pressure than the other. The giant finally broke off, laughing in delight at the stalemate.

"I am called Mikhail and you are one strong dude. Is that not what you say out West?"

"I'm no dude," Slocum said, not taking offense. Whatever language the man spoke natively, it wasn't English. From the heavy accent and his dress, Slocum decided that he must be Russian.

"I want to be dude. I want to be cowboy."

"What about that drink?" Slocum asked, not caring what Mikhail's ambitions were.

"I am Russian," Mikhail said proudly, confirming Slocum's guess. "I look for gold and adventure."

"My name's Slocum and I'm looking for a friend," he said, not knowing why he bothered mentioning this to the Russian. He sipped at the drink Mikhail had bought and nodded approvingly. The whiskey here was smoother and less potent than the brandy served on the other side of town.

"I know many here. I keep eye open all the time," Mikhail said. "Who is it you hunt?"

"His name's Scoggins. Matt Scoggins."

Mikhail furrowed his beetle brow and pursed his lips. Then he frowned even more and made a grunting sound.

"This Scoggins. He is shorter than you, bald and has scar about here?" Mikhail moved his stubby finger along the line of his chin, just above the jawbone.

This got Slocum's attention.

"You know him?"

"I have seen him." The Russian turned dour and looked away from Slocum.

"Can you tell me where he is?"

"I like you, Slocum. If you are his friend, you should know."

"Know what? Can you take me to him?"

"*Da,*" Mikhail said. He knocked back his whiskey, belched and then pointed to Slocum's drink. Slocum hastily downed what remained. "We go."

"Is it far?" Slocum would have worried about an ambush if Mikhail had not so accurately described Scoggins.

"Not far," Mikhail said. As he walked down the street, his long stride devouring distance, he fell silent. No amount of questioning could get so much as a grunt from the huge Russian. Slocum kept up, almost running, then saw the direction they were going and went cold inside.

"There," Mikhail said. "I will show you."

Slocum hesitated at the gate leading into the Goldust

cemetery. If saloons and cathouses were the first to show
up in a boomtown, cemeteries were always quick on their
heels. He went past the Masonic section of the graveyard
and followed Mikhail as he hiked up a short path to the
top of a barren hill littered with crude wooden crosses.
Mikhail stopped and pointed at one.

Slocum caught his breath. He made out his friend's
name cut into the wooden cross. There wasn't anything
else.

"What happened to him? Do you know? If somebody
murdered him, I want to know." Slocum watched Mikhail's reaction, the fleeting thought crossing his mind that
Mikhail might have ended Scoggins's life. But the giant's
expression was one of sorrow, nothing more.

"I know him a little. Not much."

"How'd he die?"

"It is not for me to say such things," Mikhail said. He
stumbled when Slocum grabbed a handful of furred coat
and shoved. He was in no mood to play games.

"Tell me what you know."

Mikhail looked at him with a combination of surprise
and awe.

"You do not fear Mikhail?"

"Matt Scoggins was my friend. If some son of a bitch
murdered him, I want to know. And if you're the one who
killed him, I'll cut out your liver and make you eat it."

"You are not afraid of me!" For Mikhail this seemed
an incredible revelation. Then the darkness of spirit settled
on him again. "I cannot tell you but my employer can. I
take you now."

"Who do you work for?" Slocum asked, but he was
speaking to the Russian's back. Mikhail already lumbered
off in the direction of Goldust, leaving Slocum to trail
behind. Slocum touched the butt of his six-gun and wondered if he ought to go along or demand an explanation
here and now. Men died all the time on the frontier, and

Scoggins always pushed people a bit too hard and too far. Such an abrasive personality was bound to bring him to a violent end. But Slocum wanted to know the details.

As he trailed Mikhail, he came to the conclusion that the Russian had nothing to do with Scoggins's death. If he had killed him, why show Slocum the grave? Why even admit knowing Scoggins? Slocum had failed to find anyone else in Goldust who even recognized the name of his former partner.

The puzzle goaded Slocum into doing as the Russian asked. For now.

Mikhail came to a halt and stood at military attention in front of the only decent hotel in Goldust. He pointed to the second story where a light burned in a front window.

"My employer's room. Come. I show you."

"You're sure he can tell me what I want to know?" asked Slocum. "I'm not in the mood for a wild goose chase."

Mikhail looked at him strangely, then laughed. Slocum couldn't tell why.

"This is not the chasing of a goose. Come." Mikhail waved a huge hand, urging Slocum to come along. They tromped through the lobby, leaving muddy tracks behind.

Slocum noticed the clerk started to protest, then saw Mikhail and clamped his mouth shut before coming around with a dustpan and short broom to clean up the dirt.

Mikhail's weight caused the stairs to creak ominously, but the giant of a man stopped at the top of the stairs in front of the first door. He pointed silently, then waited until Slocum nodded once to show that he wanted to continue. Mikhail knocked and called out something in guttural Russian. Slocum couldn't make out the muffled answer, but Mikhail opened the door and ushered Slocum inside.

Slocum stopped dead in his tracks and stared at the starkly beautiful woman sitting at the writing desk.

"My employer," Mikhail said, trying not to laugh as he bowed low in the woman's direction. "Duchess Anastasia Zharkov, cousin of our illustrious Czar Alexander the Second, and noble defender of the Russian Empire."

4

"You're Mikhail's boss?" Slocum asked, trying not to openly gawk.

The dark-haired woman looked down a short, straight nose at him, her intense dark eyes dancing with an amusement Slocum did not share. She pursed rouged lips, then carefully put down her fountain pen on the writing desk. The duchess moved to cover the letter, but Slocum already had glanced at it and had seen only the curious curlicue Russian characters. Even if he could have deciphered it, he had no knowledge of the Russian language.

"Mikhail, why do you bring this . . . one?" She leaned back indolently in her chair as her ebony eyes raked Slocum, taking in every detail of his filthy boots all the way to the patches falling off his Stetson, frozen out by the foul weather.

"Duchess Anastasia, he is friend of Scoggins. I show him grave."

"Ah, you knew Mr. Scoggins well?"

"He wrote me a letter saying he was onto a rich strike. We'd been partners before but had drifted apart."

"Ah, yes the western drifter," she said mockingly. "Is that you or Mr. Scoggins?"

"Both. What do you know about how he died? Mikhail said you would tell me."

"Speak when you are spoken to," Anastasia said testily.

"Tell me what I want to know or—"

"Or what?" she said, her dark eyes catching the fire of anger now. "You will make me? With Mikhail standing here?"

"He's a big man," Slocum said carefully, holding his own anger in check. "I'd hate to hurt him. Better tell me what I want to know. What happened to Matt Scoggins?"

"Hurt Mikhail? That is rich!" Her anger changed mercurially to humor. She laughed, but it was artificial. Anastasia Zharkov never took her gaze off Slocum, making him feel like a bug being studied intently by a dispassionate scientist.

"I remove him, Duchess," Mikhail said.

Slocum knew the giant bodyguard spoke for his benefit. Otherwise, the exchange would have been in Russian. Reaching the end of his patience, Slocum half turned, feinted right, then swung with all his might and landed his left fist in the Russian's solar plexus. He knew better than to aim for the bearded lantern jaw where he might break his knuckles or the belly that undoubtedly was so heavily muscled that it would be like striking an oak plank.

For a moment, Mikhail stood stock-still. Then he let out a tiny *woof!* and simply sat down. His eyes glazed over, and his lips moved but no sound came out. A few twitches showed he was still alive but not up to fighting Slocum.

Slocum turned back to the duchess and said, "You were telling me about Scoggins."

Anastasia's eyes had gone wide with surprise seeing how quickly her bodyguard had been felled.

"No one has ever done that to Mikhail. He is a Cossack. He is strong enough to carry his horse on his shoulders for a mile. He has killed a hundred men. He—"

"Scoggins," Slocum said.

The lovely woman smiled. "You have earned this knowledge with your bravery, Mr. Slocum. Mikhail saw something in you. I see so much more. I can understand why Mr. Scoggins considered you a friend. He was in my employ," she said, hurrying on with her explanation before Slocum could object to her roundabout recitation.

"Scoggins was more likely to hold up a gold shipment on a stage than work as a bodyguard," Slocum said. "Even for a body as attractive as yours."

"Ah," she said, melting a little more. "I wondered if you noticed."

Slocum kept quiet. He couldn't help noticing how her breasts rose and fell more quickly under her ornately embroidered vest. Her trim waist was circled by a thick belt of leather so soft Slocum fancied it might feel like butter under his fingers. She wore a flaring skirt that had been split for riding, though he could only guess since she still sat close up at the writing desk. He reckoned she would have a mighty fine set of legs, if he ever got a look.

"Mr. Scoggins was hired as a guide. He had intimate knowledge of this land that I required. Mikhail is good for many services, but this is a barren, wild land."

"Where'd you want him to guide you?" Slocum had the sinking feeling Anastasia had employed Scoggins to find her a gold mine or something equally romantic—and ridiculous.

"I am a tourist in this wild country of yours. Every detail I want to see. When I return to the czar's Winter Palace at St. Petersburg, I will be the center of the court with my tales of this wilderness."

"What did you want Scoggins to show you?" Slocum was at a loss to understand now. As lovely as the duchess was, Matt Scoggins would never have agreed to guide her on a sightseeing tour, unless the money had been outrageously good. In that case, he would never have written to Slocum asking him to come north. He would have kept it all for himself.

Whatever Scoggins had done, it had gotten him killed.

"Why, everything. The buffalo herds. Red-skinned savages. I had not expected him to show us so dangerous a crime by being a victim. He was, I believe this is the word, bushwhacked by road agents."

"Shot from ambush?"

"Yes, exactly. There was nothing Mikhail could do. We brought back the body and gave him a small burial in the cemetery. Did you realize there are no Russian Orthodox priests in this uncivilized land?"

"Scoggins wasn't likely to appreciate any man of the cloth saying words over him. Not the way he lived." Slocum thought hard. "Do you have any notion who gunned him down?"

"A man with an old musket was seen running away on foot, but more likely the killers were two men with modern rifles. Mikhail chased and saw them, but they escaped him on horseback. That is all I know. The death happened quite suddenly." Anastasia leaned forward, her eyes unreadable now. "I would hire you as guide. The pay is quite . . . substantial."

"I'm more interested in tracking the men who killed Scoggins. I owe him that much. Since there's no law in these parts, somebody's got to bring his murderers to justice."

On the floor behind him, Slocum heard Mikhail beginning to gasp as his senses returned. Slocum turned and held out his hand, helping the giant to his feet. Mikhail wobbled a little, then strengthened. The look of chagrin on his face was almost comical as he rattled off a long string of Russian to the duchess.

Slocum didn't have to understand the language to know

Mikhail was apologizing for getting decked like he had been.

Anastasia's sharp command silenced him.

"Mikhail is quite contrite about allowing you to fell him as you did," Anastasia said.

"He didn't let me do anything," Slocum said.

"The rugged frontiersman. You intrigue me, Mr. Slocum. Accept my employment. Five hundred dollars."

The amount startled Slocum. "That what you offered Scoggins?"

"No, he accepted far less. I know the worth of a man. You deserve more."

"Show me where he was shot, let me track the killers and then we'll dicker."

"Done!" Anastasia laughed delightedly. "At first light, present yourself in the lobby and we shall depart then." When Slocum hesitated, Anastasia asked, "Have you a place to stay?"

"It's a ways off. Up on Polecat Ridge."

"The abandoned line shacks?" Anastasia laughed again.

Slocum looked at the duchess with newfound curiosity. She had taken the time to learn the lay of the land around Goldust. While acting like a willful heiress out on a lark, she had absorbed a great deal of the geography. The two didn't jibe. Slocum wondered which was the real Anastasia Zharkov—the jaded tourist or the astute observer who painstakingly learned every detail around her.

"Mikhail, show Mr. Slocum to one of the rooms. The one at the end of the hall in the back should do."

"Yes, Duchess." Mikhail bowed slightly, pushed open the door and let Slocum out into the hall before pointing.

"That's my room?" Slocum asked, eyeing the other half dozen locked doors. "Who's in the others?"

"No one. Duchess Anastasia rented entire hotel. She likes privacy."

Slocum let out a deep sigh. Anastasia *was* a spoiled, rich tourist.

Slocum slept like a rock on the soft bed with the warm comforter to keep away the chill. Unlike the night before with Elizabeth Bartlett, he was curiously at ease. Why he felt this way was something of a mystery since he had learned Scoggins had been cut down by road agents, buried in a pauper's grave by a woman who obviously had an immense fortune to play with and who treated everyone like a servant.

Still, something about Anastasia Zharkov struck Slocum as different. And although he ought to have worried about angering Mikhail with the way he had felled him using a single punch, he didn't. Slocum didn't even bother locking the door leading out into the hallway.

He awoke just before dawn, stretched and went to the window. The storm that had dogged his way into Goldust had blown over and left the sky dotted with only a cloud or two. Daybreak would bring a warm sun to melt the snow and turn the land into one giant bog. Slocum wanted to reach the place where Scoggins had been shot before this happened. He might not find anything because of the snow dumped by the blizzard, but all traces would be melted away into sloppy mud in a few hours.

A quick, hard rap on his door caused him to turn, hand resting on the butt of his six-shooter. The door opened and Mikhail's bearded face thrust through.

"We go now. The duchess is ready," Mikhail said.

"Wait," Slocum called as the huge man started to retreat. "No hard feelings?"

"About what? You punch good. Mikhail strong. You are stronger, no matter that you are so teeny. You get this way from punching the cows all day and night!"

Slocum had to smile at this and was relieved when Mikhail's booming laugh rumbled through the room.

"No hard feelings," Mikhail said. "Unless you don't come now. Duchess Anastasia is impatient about hitting the road. That is the right words to say?"

Slocum nodded assent as he pulled on his duster. Unlike the night before, it wasn't frozen solid and fell loosely around him. He followed Mikhail down the steps to the lobby where Anastasia stood decked out in a flashy riding costume decorated in red silk. She tapped a short riding crop against the palm of her left hand, showing her impatience.

"You finally arrived. If you are to work for me, you must always be prompt, Mr. Slocum."

"Never said I'd work for you. First, I want to look over where Scoggins died. From what I find there, I'll make my decision."

"The snowstorm will have hidden the tracks of the killers," Anastasia said. "Mikhail tried to follow and could not. He is most expert."

From the corner of his eye Slocum saw how Mikhail puffed up at this praise from the duchess. The man was completely devoted to Anastasia and would kill for her—or die. Slocum liked Mikhail and hoped nothing came between them again. A fight to the death with the bulky Russian wasn't something he would look forward to.

Slocum fetched his horse and took a few minutes to be sure it got fodder while Anastasia and Mikhail tended their horses, a pair of powerful black stallions outfitted with fine saddles chased with silver and ornamented as if she were the czarina.

"The sun's coming up," Slocum said.

"Then we should ride as if we mean it. The spot is not so far away. Only a few miles." With that, Anastasia used her riding crop to get her magnificent stallion galloping off, Mikhail right behind.

Slocum followed at a more leisurely pace, not wanting to tire his horse needlessly. He could not expect to gallop for miles without the mare dying under him from exhaustion, and he doubted Anastasia and Mikhail would maintain their gait long. And they didn't. He caught up to them two miles down the road. Mikhail looked upset at him, and Slocum couldn't tell what emotions bubbled and boiled under Anastasia's studied, cool exterior.

"You did not keep up with us. You fell behind," she accused.

"My horse isn't any match for yours," Slocum said. "Is this the spot?" If he were to ambush anyone, he couldn't have picked a finer location. Trees to one side of the road afforded cover for a small army of snipers. The road bent in a hairpin turn, forcing any rider to turn attention to the road and away from the countryside. If Scoggins had been riding toward Goldust, he would have exposed his back to a gunman hiding in a thick copse not thirty yards away.

"It is," Mikhail said, then fell silent when Anastasia's cold look told him he spoke out of turn.

"Yes, we were—" she started.

"You were heading to town and the killers shot Scoggins in the back," Slocum said, his anger a cold flame inside. "They fired from there."

"How do you know this? You were not here!" exclaimed Mikhail.

Slocum didn't bother explaining. His checkered past had more than its share of outlawry in it. If he had wanted to kill a rider, that was precisely what he would have done.

"Wait here. I'll see what I can find."

"Go with him, Mikhail," ordered Anastasia. To Slocum she said, "He is an excellent tracker. The best."

Slocum shrugged it off. As long as Mikhail didn't obliterate whatever faint traces might remain, he was welcome. Slocum rode halfway to the stand of juniper trees, then dismounted. He preferred to examine the terrain on foot. Mikhail silently followed his lead.

Slocum stopped at the edge of the thicket. Slowly pacing back and forth, he studied the shrubs until he came to one and stared at it.

"There are no tracks in snow," Mikhail said.

"But there is a broken twig on that bush. It's started to die. It'd take about a week for it to wither the way it has."

"That is when Scoggins died," Mikhail confirmed.

"The sniper stood there," Slocum said, advancing cautiously, "broke the twig and then rested his rifle in the notch. See the scrape marks left by the front barrel?"

Mikhail muttered to himself as he peered over Slocum's shoulder. He doubted Slocum's evidence but said nothing aloud. For Slocum's part, there was no question about what had happened. The junipers had blocked much of the snowfall from the blizzard, permitting only a light dusting of flakes to settle down. Slocum's keen eyes spotted faint depressions in the snow where the new fall had filled boot prints and hoofprints.

He rounded the shrub with the broken twig and paralleled the tracks. Mikhail grumbled about finding nothing but came along. Slocum ignored the giant Russian and concentrated on the tracks, which became fainter as they went into the thicket.

More on faith than skill, Slocum continued through the stand of junipers until he came to the far side. Here the land had been exposed to the full fury of the blizzard. Any hope for tracking was long erased, but Slocum refused to give up. He climbed to the top of a small hill and looked around.

"What's in that direction?" he asked Mikhail.

"Deadwood. More than fifteen miles."

"That's where I'll find Scoggins's killers. They lay in wait, shot him and then lit out for Deadwood."

"You know all this from nothing? I am the best tracker on the steppes and I see nothing."

"The steppes are different from Dakota Territory," Slocum said. He could have shown the traces he had seen, but the sun was well above the treetops now, delivering rays of warmth to the ground for the first time in days. Already the snow was slumping down into a crust, effectively removing what small prints Slocum had found.

He returned to the spot where the gunmen had waited and carefully looked around, then shoved his hand down into the snow and came up with a shiny brass cartridge.

"How many times did the sniper shoot?" Slocum asked.

"Once."

Slocum's resolve hardened. Whoever had lain in wait hadn't intended to kill the duchess or her bodyguard. They had shot Scoggins, then left, their job done. Matt Scoggins had been the intended victim. Otherwise, more rounds would have been fired.

"When I find the rifle that fired this shell, I'll have the weapon used to kill Scoggins. And when I put the rifle in the hands of its owner, I'll be face to face with his killer."

Slocum tucked the shell into his vest pocket, then closed his duster and returned to the road where Anastasia waited restlessly with his and Mikhail's horses. Slocum had two killers to track down. The sooner he started, the better his chances of bringing some justice to Goldust—and Matt Scoggins.

5

"Now that you are done poking about in the musty forest," Anastasia began, "you will escort me to a mining camp. I would see how gold is made."

"Sorry, Duchess," Slocum said, cutting her off. "I found where two men lay in ambush for Scoggins."

"He found shell casing," Mikhail said glumly.

"But Mikhail, you found nothing when you looked before," Anastasia said, startled. "How did he do this?"

Slocum held down his irritation at the way the duchess spoke to Mikhail about him, as if he weren't even there. He had made up his mind, so it really didn't matter how she treated him or spoke about him. Some folks had been far ruder to Slocum—and they were nowhere near as pretty as Anastasia Zharkov.

"You tell her what went on, Mikhail," Slocum said. "I'll let you know how my hunt comes out."

"Wait!" Anastasia's command was so sharp that Slocum bristled. He was no servant to be ordered about.

"I said I'll let you know when the men who killed Scoggins are buzzard bait," he said as cold as any wind blowing off the nearby snowbanks. His green eyes locked with Anastasia's dark ones in a battle of wills. Slocum wasn't going to lose, and the Russian duchess quickly realized it.

"I am sorry. I did not mean to sound so, so abrupt. It is my manner. You are a clever man and well skilled in the ways of the frontier. I seek only to find new experiences. Could I ride with you on your hunt for these killers? Mr. Scoggins was an employee at the time, and I feel some obligation."

Slocum knew a lie when he heard it. Whatever Anastasia felt had nothing to do with the responsibility of an employer toward an employee. He had seen and heard the same bullshit from slave owners before the war.

"Please, Mr. Slocum," Anastasia said, seeing that her plea fell on deaf ears. "Mikhail is an excellent fighter. You might find these men and need his abilities." Anastasia smiled winningly and added, "Who knows? You might find you need mine, as well."

Slocum held back from asking what abilities she meant.

"This is a free country. You can ride along, if you like. Nothing's going to get in the way of me finding them."

"You are such a determined man," Anastasia said. "I like that. I, too, am determined."

"To enjoy a vacation in the American West, no matter how many men die?" Slocum asked. But he had heard something more in the way the duchess spoke. He got conflicting impressions of her. This time all trace of spoiled, rich royalty was lacking and an iron core of resolve tinged her words. She sought something as surely as he did. But what? Slocum's curiosity wasn't going to get the better of him until he had found Scoggins's killers. Afterward?

The duchess was a lovely woman.

"Of course I care if men die," she said too quickly.

Slocum set out on the road toward Deadwood, keenly aware of the exquisite duchess riding at his side. If he intended to get into the rough-and-tumble town without creating a fuss, he had to leave Anastasia behind. Or perhaps he could use her beauty as a diversion. His brain turned over one scheme after another, but he had to admit he was coming up as dry as a West Texas water well on how to find the men who had killed his partner. Time and weather had removed all but the most obvious traces of the week-old trail.

He needed descriptions of the killers before he could do anything more. Coming to this realization rankled, especially now that Anastasia and Mikhail rode with him. Slocum wasn't inclined to give up, but his options were limited having them with him.

"There, Mr. Slocum. That awful, muddy trail leading into the hills goes to a gold mine, doesn't it?"

"Probably," Slocum said, distracted.

"Could it be that the proprietors of such a mine saw the men ride past who killed your friend?" asked Anastasia. "Knowing what they looked like, how they dressed, some small item about them other than they are expert with rifles would be of use finding them, would it not?"

"You want to see a mine, don't you?" asked Slocum. He grinned ruefully. Anastasia had a way about her. She turned her desires into a command he wanted to obey.

"If it would help bring Mr. Scoggins's murderers to justice, why, yes, naturally I would."

Slocum judged where the two might have gone on their way to Deadwood, if they had gone to that town at all, and decided there was a possibility miners could have spotted them. The sound of a rifle shot wouldn't have alerted miners as much as riders on their claim.

Tugging at the reins, Slocum got his mare moving up the treacherously slippery muddy trail to the Big Nugget Mine, or so it said on a poorly lettered sign near the road. Slocum knew how touchy miners were about claim jumpers so he rode slowly, making no effort at keeping quiet or staying out of sight. Anastasia chattered on blithely about everything she had seen already on her trip to the wilderness, and Mikhail rode stoically, eyes ahead.

"Hold up," Slocum said. "Something's wrong."

"What could possibly be wrong on such a fine day?" asked the duchess.

"Someone's watching us," Slocum said. He had the feeling of eyes trained on him—on them. He turned in the saddle to look back down the road to see if anyone had followed them when he caught the glint of sunlight off the front sight of a rifle.

"Mikhail, down!" Slocum shouted. The Russian reacted instantly and saved his own life doing so. The bullet intended for his broad back ripped through the air inches above him as he dived from the back of his stallion. The Russian hit the ground with a grunt, rolled and came to a sitting position. From somewhere in the depths of his fur coat he drew a pair of pistols. He had them out but had no idea where his ambusher was.

Slocum got his horse between the sniper and Anastasia as he pulled his own Winchester from the saddle sheath. He realized he had not cleaned the grease and oil off the rifle when he went to lever a round into the chamber. The cold grease prevented him from successfully chambering a round. Slocum shoved the rifle back angrily and drew his six-gun.

"There," he called to Mikhail. "Downhill and to the left." He raised his Colt Navy and got off a round where he had seen the rifle barrel poking out into the sunlight. His shot kicked up a plume of snow from a snowbank, but he didn't have a clear view of the ambusher.

Mikhail got to his feet, roared like a lion and charged toward the spot.

"Stop, don't!" cried Slocum. He spun and snapped at Anastasia, "He'll listen to you. Tell him to stop."

"It is too late. His honor is offended," she said, almost

offhandedly. "He will kill the man who tried to murder him."

"The hell he will," growled Slocum. He put his heels to his mare's flanks and got the horse loping over the rugged ground, following the angry Russian toward the black piles of tailings from the mine. Somewhere in that gravelly maze hid a killer.

The thought came to Slocum that it might be the same backshooter who had ended Matt Scoggins's life. If a miner had gone trigger-happy and was afraid anyone coming along the road was a claim jumper, he might open fire indiscriminately. Even as the idea occurred, it died. That made no sense. Why kill only Scoggins and not take potshots at Anastasia and Mikhail? The Russians had definitely said a single shot had been fired, killing Scoggins. If a crazed miner thought they were after his claim, he would have kept firing until they were all dead.

Unless Scoggins's death wasn't as they had told him. Had the duchess and her servant turned tail and run?

Slocum didn't believe that was too likely, either, not from the bullheaded way Mikhail charged at the sniper trying to shoot him in the back. Whether it came from bravery or stupidity, Mikhail wasn't the sort to act like a craven.

Slocum's horse began picking her way through the rubble, wary of stepping into a hole. Seeing the danger, Slocum jumped to the ground and let the horse make her way back off the littered hillside. The gold mine higher on the hill had spewed forth tailings for months, leaving a web of rock big enough to step on and turn an ankle.

"Mikhail!" Slocum shouted. He cocked his head to one side and listened hard. He expected to hear the huge Russian blundering around, but he didn't. Only the soft whine of wind blowing from higher on the slope came to his ears. No Russian, no bushwhacker.

Slocum grumbled to himself, then got down to tracking.

He quickly discovered the rock didn't give any clues at all to the Russian's course, or that of the man who had tried to backshoot him. This worried Slocum more and more as he wandered around. No scent, no sound, not even a flash of movement warned of a trap—or Mikhail's dead body.

Wherever the Russian and his quarry had gone was beyond the side of the hill. Slocum knew he would eventually find them, but he stopped and looked at his back trail. Leaving Anastasia alone rankled. The ambush might have been an attempt to separate her from the two men most likely to defend her.

Slocum took a final look into the head-high piles of black tailings, then retraced his steps to the muddy road leading up to the main mine shaft. His heart jumped into his throat when he saw Anastasia's horse standing beside a shack. The duchess was nowhere to be seen.

He started to call out, then thought better of it. He made a beeline for the cabin, checked the horse to see if there was any hint of a fight, then stepped to the rickety door.

"Duchess?" he called. "You inside?"

He didn't hesitate. He had warned her he was coming. Kicking in the door with a loud bang, he jumped in, his six-shooter leveled and ready to shoot anyone holding her hostage. Slocum released the hammer and let it down gently when he saw her sitting elegantly at a battered table, a tin cup in front of her.

"The coffee was still warm. I thought to have a cup. Would you like to share mine?" she asked, holding up the cup. "There is not a second cup."

"I couldn't find Mikhail."

"Do not worry so about him, Mr. Slocum. He is a veteran soldier and knows the way of battle."

"He risked his life and yours running off the way he did."

"My life? I am in no danger. Am I?" Her ebony eyes fixed on him.

"Not from me," Slocum said, "but somebody killed Scoggins while you were riding with him, and now somebody tried to gun down Mikhail."

"How can you be so sure the unseen gunman wasn't shooting at you?" She daintily picked up the cup and sipped at it. She made a face as she put the cup back on the table. "The coffee is weak. I prefer Turkish coffee. It is very strong."

Slocum ignored her preferences in coffee and thought about where they had been on the road when the sniper had fired. He realized he might have been the target rather than Mikhail, but he didn't think so. The killer had a chance to shoot him a minute earlier, taking an easier shot. Or had the ambusher only arrived?

There was too much Slocum didn't know, and he knew too little about the duchess and her reasons for prowling around Goldust.

"You should head on back to town and let me find Mikhail," Slocum said.

"The weather is turning foul. I might not make it all the way to Goldust before the storm strikes."

Slocum frowned. He hadn't noticed the weather changing again. Poking his head out and looking to the north, he realized he had been too intent on finding Mikhail and the man who had tried to dry-gulch him. The quickness with which a new storm built told him how deadly Dakota Territory could be in the winter.

"We can make it back, if we hurry."

"What of Mikhail? He is still on foot. You return to Goldust, Mr. Slocum. I shall stay and wait for him to find me." The way Anastasia phrased her words so carefully were designed to prevent Slocum from doing any such thing. He could not abandon her. Even if it were in his nature, leaving now made it appear as if he was a coward running for shelter.

"Have you looked around the mine?" he asked. His sudden turn startled her.

"Why, yes, I have. There seems little activity here any longer. I have viewed the area of gold removal in the mine walls and the vats where acid was applied to separate the gold from the dross. It was most enlightening."

Slocum reached out and put a hand against a cabin wall when a sudden gust of wind threatened to cave it in. He knew that any chance of getting back to Goldust before the storm hit was lost now.

"I'll stable the horses inside the mine. If this shack starts to fall apart, we might have to join them."

"Very well, Mr. Slocum. Do hurry back."

He stared at her, wondering at the change in her tone.

"The weather is getting colder. You must remain . . . warm."

Slocum was buffeted by the rising storm wind as he led their horses into the mouth of the mine. It was cold inside but gave shelter from the wind. He considered moving here and spreading his bedroll near the animals to keep them calm, but none of them seemed too spooked by being sheltered in a mine shaft.

He pressed his hat hard into his head, tucked his chin to his chest and braved the gale-force winds whipping through the deserted mining camp. It was a physical relief when he pushed the cabin door shut and leaned against it. Not only was he out of the wind but Anastasia had built a fire in the Franklin stove, warming the cabin considerably.

"Come, sit by the roaring fire," she said sardonically. "It will warm your bones."

"We'll have to ride out the storm," he said. "Mikhail might not be lucky enough to survive."

"He is strong. He is a Cossack. It will take more than this pitiful chill to kill him."

"I wouldn't call it pitiful. That's a powerful cold wind blowing, and I smell snow on it."

"Winter in Russia is fiercer." She laughed, and it sounded like silver cathedral bells tolling. "*Spring* in Russia is worse."

Slocum spread his bedroll near the stove and warmed his hands. Anastasia sat beside him, unbothered by the razor-edged wind or the steadily dropping temperatures.

"You cannot find the men who killed your friend unless you know more about them," Anastasia pointed out. "Why not guide me through the West for a few days? The trail, as I think you say, will not be any colder if you wait."

She rested her hand on his arm. He felt her warm fingers—and more. He turned toward the dark-haired beauty and stared into her fathomless eyes. He knew she had a way of getting what she wanted. It just happened that both of them wanted the same thing right now. Slocum bent down and kissed her on her full, ruby-tinted lips.

Slocum was pleasantly surprised at the passion he unlocked in her. The simple kiss turned more intense until they were both gasping for breath. Slocum felt her breasts crushing against his chest as she strained to get ever closer.

When Anastasia's lips parted slightly, Slocum invaded Russian territory. His tongue surged out and dueled erotically with hers. She caught his tongue between her white teeth and bit down lightly, running her own tongue along the tip of his. Then her tongue rushed into his mouth where they played hide and seek.

Slocum's hands began to roam down the woman's strong arms and around, down her back and finally low enough to cup her buttocks. Anastasia rose off the floor slightly and allowed Slocum to work his hand fully under

her. He began kneading the fleshy orbs hidden under her
riding skirts. He felt a new level of response in her body.

"More," she whispered hotly in his ear before nibbling
on it. "Give me more. Give it all to me!"

This was an order Slocum willingly obeyed. He slid his
hands between them so he could begin unfastening the
ties on Anastasia's blouse. The frilly undergarment was
more of a challenge, but he was up to it. Soon enough
her snowy-white, firm breasts tumbled out into his palms.
He cupped those succulent globes and pressed hard. He
felt the tiny pink buttons capping each breast begin to
pulse with need.

He kissed her lips and cheeks and eyes and then worked
to her throat. Anastasia threw her head back to fully expose her swan-like throat to his kisses. Then he worked
lower into the canyon between her towering breasts. Slocum licked and kissed and lightly nipped at the soft,
tender flesh before spiraling upward to the summit of the
left tit.

His lips caught at the hard nubbin he found there and
sucked it into his mouth. He used his teeth on the throb-
bing button of flesh the same way she had attacked his
tongue when he had invaded her mouth. The response this
time was different, though.

"Oh, John, yes, oh, yes!" she gasped out. Anastasia
murmured more in Russian that he didn't understand.
What Slocum did know was that she needed more than
he was giving.

He abandoned her left nipple and went directly to the
right one, giving it the same treatment. The bumpy plain
surrounding the nipple began to throb with every frenzied
beat of the Russian noblewoman's heart. He shoved his
tongue out hard, pushing the nub down into the soft flesh
beneath. This caused Anastasia to arch her back and try
to shove her entire beast into his mouth.

Slocum kissed and licked and nibbled more before

moving lower on her body. Her heaving belly was exposed after he got the ties unfastened at her waist. She wiggled about and kicked hard to get free of the rest of her undergarments. Anastasia lay back completely naked, white flesh gleaming in the pale light from the stone. Nestled between her ivory thighs was a dark triangle of fleece that drew Slocum like a magnet draws iron.

He touched that furry patch, then curled a finger up into her steamy interior. Anastasia lay back, supporting herself on her elbows. She lifted her legs and spread them in wanton invitation.

Slocum ran his finger in and out of her a few times, then dipped down and used his tongue where his finger had gone. Anastasia cried out in delight at this gentle intrusion. Her hands came down so her fingers laced through his thick hair. She held his face in place as he continued to lave and lick and thrust with his tongue.

A deep shudder passed through the woman's trim body, then she relaxed a little.

In a husky voice she said, "Now I want you. You!"

Slocum stood and quickly shucked off his shirt, kicked free of his boots and began working down his trousers. The duchess swarmed up and helped. Gone was all her sophisticated attitude. Replacing it was pure lust.

She brushed Slocum's manhood across her lips, then fell onto her back, her legs wider than before.

"Now, John, now is the time. Hurry!"

The wind beat a crescendo against the walls, rising and falling powerfully. Slocum dropped down and let her guide him to the spot they both desired filled. The tip of his rigid shaft touched her dampened nether lips, then he plunged forward balls-deep.

They both cried out at the sudden intrusion so far into her clutching sheath. Slocum was surrounded by moist, pressing female flesh. And then he withdrew slowly. Anastasia shuddered as every inch disappeared from her.

When only the thick arrowhead of his rod remained within her, Slocum paused to get his breath, then rushed back to fill her to overflowing.

Faster and faster he moved. Friction burned them delightfully. Convulsive shudders of desire racked Anastasia repeatedly and soon Slocum began feeling the heat building in his own loins turn to a raging forest fire beyond control.

He thrust harder, faster, deeper, and then it was over in a fierce rush. Sweating, he sank down on her naked body. Anastasia put her arms around him and rolled to one side so they could lie nearer the fire.

Even so, Slocum felt the wintery cold against exposed portions of his anatomy.

"What's wrong? Getting cold again so soon?" joked Anastasia. "I know the way to rob the storm of its due."

She began showing him how a Russian defeated the long, cold winter nights. Slocum approved.

6

The fire had died in the stove, leaving the cabin cold and dark. Slocum rubbed his eyes, then sat up. It felt as if someone pulled an icy rake across his bare flesh. He shivered as he reached for his clothing. Fumbling around in his vest pocket, Slocum found the only legacy left him by his brother, Robert, who had died during Pickett's Charge. Slocum opened the watch case and turned the face so he could make out the time. What he read startled him.

He held the watch to his ear to be sure it was still running.

Either he and Anastasia had put in a powerful lot of loving in only an hour or it was past ten in the morning.

Beside him the lovely Russian duchess stirred, then rolled over to continue her deep sleep. A creamy white shoulder gleamed like alabaster in the dark. Slocum reached over and pulled the blanket up over her bare flesh, wanting to delve farther under the wool blanket to find the rest of her naked, warm skin but knowing time had gotten away from him.

The whistle and whine of the wind had stopped, but the darkness bothered him. Slocum stood, dressed the best

he could and then went to the shack door and pushed. He
didn't budge the door an inch. Pressing his hand against
the wood told the story. Cold as ice. The snow had drifted
up onto the door outside and held them prisoner inside
the cabin.

Slocum wasn't too worried about this. The other side
of the cabin wouldn't have that kind of frigid weight
against it. He could always pull down a few boards or
even go through the roof. Stepping over Anastasia, he
found a knothole in the back wall and peered through it.
He drew back and poked his finger through, knocking out
an icy plug.

He caught his breath at the sight of a new two-foot
snowfall. The land looked virginal, pure and unsullied.
From his tiny peephole, he couldn't even see animal
tracks in the snow, although it was past ten in the morning. Heavy clouds hid the sun, but it was definitely day.
His watch had not lied.

"John?" Anastasia stirred. He heard her reaching out
and not finding him wrapped in the blankets beside her.

"I'm trying to figure out how to get out of the cabin.
The snow drifted against the door. Digging out would be
more trouble than it's worth."

"Why leave?" she asked in a sleepy voice. "We can
while away the hours here." She clacked her teeth together
as she sat up, the chill hitting her like a fist when the
blanket slid from her upper body. In the dim light filtering
into the cabin, Slocum saw her firm, full breasts ripple
with gooseflesh from the cold. She pulled the blanket up
around her shoulders.

"We need more firewood. The horses have to be fed.
And there's the matter of Mikhail."

"What of him?" she asked. Anastasia stood, the casu-
ally draped blanket giving him delightfully revealing
glimpses of her bare body. "He is capable of taking care
of himself."

"Back on the Russian steppes, maybe," Slocum said. "Out here the rules are different."

"Not that different. Mikhail has fought Mongol hordes and bandits and even throngs of peasants with torches and pitchforks. You have no idea how ugly *they* can be," she said. Seeing that he wasn't going to be seduced into more lovemaking by revealing her nakedness in a teasing, tantalizing fashion, Anastasia began dressing. Slocum knew her every move was intended to incite him.

And it did.

He held himself in check as she slowly drew on each piece of clothing, smoothing away wrinkles and patting down the folds. Slocum turned and began tugging at the plank on the back wall. When it came free, a tiny drift of snow fell to the floor. Along with it came a gust of winter air that caused him to take a step back. He was glad Anastasia had finished dressing. Her boasts of how she endured the cold in Russia would have been put to the lie with this rush of arctic breeze.

A second board followed, allowing Slocum to crawl out onto the crusty surface of the new snowfall. He made his way to the mine, found it completely blocked, found a shovel and began digging out the mouth so he could reach the horses. To his relief they were skittish but not too spooked from being snowed into the mine.

Another hour foraging got them enough fodder to keep going. Slocum returned to the cabin, surprised to see a new curl of black smoke coming from the chimney. A heady scent of something cooking drew him back inside. Anastasia fussed over the stove, rattling an old pot with a wood spoon as she stirred vigorously.

"There was nothing in the way of food inside the cabin, so I found some roots and even a tuber to boil for breakfast. I think it might please you." She held out the wooden spoon for him to take a sip.

Once Slocum got past the boiling heat, he was surprised to find the broth to be tasty.

"You're quite a surprise, Duchess," he said. "A cook as well as royalty."

Anastasia let out a deep sigh. "I had thought you would have remembered more about my talents, after last night." She flashed him a wicked grin. "I shall work on sharp-. ening your memory, though little else of your performance requires improvement." She ladled out some of the broth into the tin cup and handed it to him.

Slocum drank greedily, the warmth spreading throughout his body. He drank a second cup, watching the duchess more carefully. She worked at appearing to be the spoiled tourist interested only in a momentary diversion, but he caught the iron beneath that facade.

"Why are you here?" he asked.

"We are snowed in, of course," she said, spooning some of the broth from the pot to her lips.

"Not here in this cabin," Slocum said impatiently. "Here in the Dakotas. There's nothing here to draw you, especially in the winter. If you wanted to visit America, you'd take in the big cities. San Francisco and St. Louis— or New York. I've heard of Russians coming to hunt buffalo, but this is a bad time for that. Spring is better."

"I am nothing more than I seem," Anastasia said.

Slocum let the matter drop. He knew a lie when he heard it, no matter how it was covered in sugary talk. When she saw he wasn't buying her tall tale, it seemed to irritate her.

"You know nothing of what life is like in Russia. This is paradise in comparison."

"Even compared to your czar's fabulous Winter Palace?" She had spoken several times of how Czar Alexander lived high on the hog during the winter while the peasants toiled to support his exuberant, lavish way of living. They starved while he enjoyed fancy dress balls and the finest of foods imported from Europe.

"Life at the czar's court can be more dangerous than being stranded in a blizzard. There are risks and risks."

"Politics," Slocum said, snorting in disgust. He realized a duchess in the Russian court had to practice the back-stabbing and gossiping to maintain her position, but it seemed beneath Anastasia. Or perhaps she was right, and he really did not know her.

"It is the way I live, John," she said. "Perhaps you would enjoy it, should you learn the benefits."

"I have to find Mikhail and be sure he's not frozen stiff in the forest. He shouldn't have run off after the sniper like he did. That was a damned fool thing to do."

"Mikhail angers easily," she said, "but he is a loyal retainer. I would not like to see any harm come to him."

Slocum finished his broth and silently handed Anastasia the tin cup. He settled his duster, wiggled through the hole he had made in the wall and, from outside, called back, "Stay here. I want to know where to find you."

"I will wait for you," she said, a gleam in her shining dark eyes. Before Slocum could move, she came to him, grabbed the collar of his duster and pulled his face to hers for a passionate kiss. "That will help you remember why you are to return safely."

"I'm not likely to forget, kiss or not," Slocum allowed. He considered getting his mare and going after Mikhail but figured the heavy snowfall might hinder the horse more than it would him on foot.

He had no trouble finding the spot where the dry-gulcher had fired. From here Slocum had to rely on his direction bump. The snow completely hid any tracks made by either Mikhail or his quarry. Walking carefully, Slocum went deeper into the juniper grove, every sense alert for trouble. He sank over the tops of his boots with every step and found himself fighting to stay upright as much

as he wanted to concentrate completely on finding Mikhail.

After an hour of tromping through the deep snow, Slocum found a rocky patch where the snow had blown
clean. The going was easier, but he had no clear idea he
was even close to Mikhail's trail—until he spotted a shining brass cartridge. The fitful sunlight had poked through
a cloud and caught a ray on the brass, then vanished behind a heavy cloud. The brief glint was enough for Slocum.

He picked up the casing and examined it. From its location he thought it was recently fired from a rifle. He sat
and pulled out the spent cartridge he had found where
Matt Scoggins had been killed and compared the two.
Slocum had hoped to find matching scratches or evidence
of the same hammer striking the primer in the base. He
gave up trying to match the two. They might have been
used in the same rifle. Or perhaps not.

Scouting the area produced nothing of interest, though
he thought he saw frozen tracks leading off the slippery
rock and going downhill. Falling to his belly, he studied
the partial track. Whether he had found Mikhail's trail or
someone else's, Slocum could not tell. But it was the only
spoor he had, so he went downslope.

Here and there he spied evidence that someone had
passed by recently. Broken twigs with snow frozen on the
torn, exposed ends, notches in tree trunks, small things—
and nothing to show it had been Mikhail who had come
this way.

Slocum resolutely pushed on until he came to a broad,
flat meadow. The first thing he noticed at the edge where
he emerged from the forest were bullet holes. The sap had
barely bubbled up to cover the wound before the storm
had struck.

He dug four rifle slugs from trees and estimated the
direction of fire. Slocum began hiking across the meadow

and found bushes trampled to the ground before getting covered by a thin dusting of snow. Here and there he saw specks of blood on limbs and branches. Five slugs in trees showed the other side of the battle.

The deformed lead might have come from a rifle or Mikhail's heavy pistols. If Mikhail had fired in this direction, his aim was better than the man he hunted. One serious wound had been inflicted and, from the amount of blood, Slocum guessed there might have been several hits.

But from here the trail vanished. Try as he might he could not find where any of the men locked in the fierce gunfight had fled.

Slocum glanced at the sky, then pulled out his watch and saw that it would be dark in another hour. He had spent most of the day tracking Mikhail, to no avail.

Knowing he shouldn't have left Anastasia alone all day, Slocum began retracing his steps to the miner's cabin. He wouldn't mind spending another night with the sexy duchess but felt the obligation to find her servant burning inside him.

Where had Mikhail gone?

7

"This is ridiculous. I shall go crazy with boredom," Anastasia Zharkov said airily, avoiding his eyes as she looked around the lobby of the Goldust hotel. She waved her long-fingered hand about. Two gold rings caught the pale sunlight angling through the plate glass window to the south. Slocum wondered if that was native gold or if she had brought the rings from Russia. Somehow, he doubted the duchess had done much casual sightseeing since arriving in Dakota Territory. Whatever she sought had nothing to do with trivial items like jewelry.

Slocum knew that Scoggins wouldn't have been sucked into anything that didn't pay well and interest him. Anastasia had offered him a bit of intrigue along with adventure—and a pile of money.

"Mikhail needs help. He was in a shoot-out with the bushwhacker. From the blood spattered all over the forest, Mikhail winged him a couple times."

"So what is the problem, Mr. Slocum?" she asked formally.

Slocum was aware of the hotel desk clerk trying to eavesdrop without giving the appearance of being too nosy. He wished Anastasia would talk in her room where there was a little more privacy, but she insisted on arguing in public.

"If Mikhail had killed his attacker, he would have returned. I saw no evidence he tried to get back to you. That means he kept after the sniper."

"It might take longer to run this jackal to ground than Mikhail thought. There is no need to worry about him. I command you to see me to—"

"I'll be back when I can," Slocum said sharply. "With Mikhail or his body."

"Wait, John!" the duchess called. "I did not mean to sound so, so—"

"So strong-willed?" Slocum said, picking the least insulting of the possibilities that came to mind.

"This is not easy for me. I am used to being obeyed without question."

"I'll be sure Mikhail remembers that," Slocum said, leaving her standing in the middle of the hotel lobby. She could follow or not, as she saw fit. Slocum thought she would not venture out until the matter of Mikhail's safety was resolved.

Slocum mounted his patiently waiting mare, sucked in a deep lungful of air freshened by the storm, then rode out of Goldust. He worried that the giant Russian was dead out in the forest and his killer, although wounded, was gloating over the death.

Somewhere in the back of his mind, Slocum had to wonder if the attempted backshooting tied in with Scoggins's death. A man willing to gun down another from hiding once would do it again. More than this, Slocum had to wonder if Scoggins had been the rifleman's real target. The backshooter might have gotten spooked when he saw that he had killed the wrong man. Following this line of reasoning meant Mikhail had been the target before. This posed other, equally unanswerable questions. Why kill him and not the duchess?

Slocum's head began to spin from too many possibilities. He dealt in hard, cold facts and had very few at the moment. Tracking down the man who had taken the potshot at Mikhail would be a start toward solving the mystery surrounding Scoggins's death.

He reached the spot in the forest dotted with blood and began searching for the direction taken by both Mikhail and his wounded quarry. Taking his time and using every bit of skill and intuition led him off to the east. When he hit a game trail that had mostly melted the snow from it, Slocum hit pay dirt. Not only did he find boot prints he recognized as Mikhail's, he also saw hoofprints. The wounded man had mounted and rode ahead of the pursuing Russian.

Slocum put his heels to his mare's flanks and got the horse moving faster. He felt he was nearing the end of his hunt.

Less than ten minutes later he felt a warm breeze against his face. Slocum reined back and looked around. The wind came from a crack in the hillside that he recognized all too well. Like the cave that had saved his life earlier, he had found yet another outlet for the endless wind from the center of the earth. The way the mud was chopped up in front of the cave told him a horse had run off to the east, probably without its rider from the way its stride showed a wild gallop, and two sets of tracks going into the cave.

Mikhail had run his sniper to ground.

Slocum held back from rushing into the cave. He studied the ground more carefully and went cold inside when he realized two sets of prints led into the cave but none came out. Patting his horse on the neck, he kept the mare quiet as he rode around the area, hoping to find some trace of the Russian or evidence that he had left the cavern.

Nothing.

Slocum rode back to the cave mouth and made certain

he hadn't missed any small clue that he was wrong about
the two men entering the cave but not leaving. As far as
he could tell, he was right. Slocum tethered his horse
nearby where it could graze on some scraggly sagebrush.
He took a deep breath, drew his six-shooter and started
into the cave. Every sense straining, Slocum stepped into
another world.

Darkness enveloped him. No musty smell reached his
nose, but he felt the warm gusts of air from the cave
interior. Slocum reckoned the small cave openings were
all connected beneath the surface in a single larger net-
work. That was the only explanation he could come up
with for so many sighing rocky holes in the ground.

The whistle of the wind covered smaller sounds, if there
were any. At the edge of light sneaking in from outside,
Slocum knelt and looked at the muddy ground. He
reached down and scooped up some dirt that had turned
to mud because of a tiny pool of blood. Wiping it off on
his duster, Slocum continued into the cave, letting the
inky blackness swallow him whole.

Slocum paused when he saw faint light ahead. He
looked up and decided there was a rocky chimney that
had broken through to the snowy landscape above the
cave. He picked up the blood trail again, then stopped a
short distance from where the hole in the rocky roof let
in a tight, small circle of light.

The darkness welled more intense at his feet. If he had
kept walking for the light he might have stepped off into
the pit. Slocum dropped to his belly and felt to determine
the limits of the hole. It stretched almost from wall to
wall, making it a deadly trap for anyone bulling through.

Like Mikhail. If his quarry had led him purposefully
into the cave and knew of the pit, he could have lured the
unsuspecting, angry Russian to his death. Slocum pulled
out a lucifer and drew it along a rough rock several times
until it flared brightly. He squinted and then turned his

gaze downward. The sputtering friction match cast dancing shadows as it burned, but Slocum saw what he had
feared.

Crumpled at the bottom of the fifteen-foot-deep hole
lay Mikhail.

Slocum didn't bother calling to the Russian. From the
way the man lay, he wasn't likely to answer. Ever. Before
the match burned out, Slocum lifted it and examined the
far lip of the pit. Bits of rock had been broken off, as if
someone had vaulted across the hole and had almost
plunged to the bottom. His quarry had vaulted the pit and
then lured Mikhail on. From the way Mikhail sprawled,
Slocum thought the Russian had jumped, slipped and
fallen to his death.

Cursing when the match burned his fingers, Slocum
dropped the burned stub into the hole. It faded to darkness
before it fell halfway to Mikhail. Slocum pushed back
from the pit, got to his feet and made his way back to the
cave opening. He moved his horse to a better patch of
buffalo grass poking through the snow, then pulled his
lariat free from his saddle.

He quickly returned to the edge of the pit, found a
stable rock and took a double turn around it before tying
a secure knot. Slocum dropped the free end of the rope
into the pit, then grabbed hold and swung out so he kept
his feet against the vertical wall. He lowered himself
quickly, walking down the sheer face until he saw Mikhail's dim form a couple feet under him. Slocum dropped
the last few feet to land in a crouch beside the dead Russian.

"No matter what Anastasia says," Slocum muttered,
"you were a fool. You let him lure you into a trap." Grunting, Slocum rolled over the body so it laid on its back.

For a moment, Slocum thought his eyes tricked him.
He got out another lucifer and lit it, bending down to
examine Mikhail's belly. He straightened as the match

burned out. Slocum had been wrong about Mikhail. The man hadn't died from the fall into the pit. Someone had efficiently gutted him with a knife and then dumped his body into this hole.

The small amount of blood under the body confirmed it. Mikhail had been killed somewhere else and then dumped after he was dead—dead men didn't bleed. Slocum frowned. Was the trail of blood leading into the cave Mikhail's? Somehow, he doubted it. The trap made more sense if it had been set up differently. Mikhail had chased the man who had tried to ambush him. The blood came from the Russian giant's quarry, who decoyed him into the cave. Mikhail had not fallen into the pit but had jumped it, maybe barely making the jump in time. Slocum had not checked the far side of the pit to see if there was more blood there, wrongly thinking Mikhail had fallen to his death.

Mikhail had made the jump, been knifed and died. Then he had been pushed into the pit to get rid of his body.

"Why get rid of the body?" Slocum wondered to himself. "Who'd ever see it?" Cold realization drove into him as painful as the knife had been for Mikhail. Slocum grabbed for the rope and started clambering up when he heard the soft scrape of boots against rock.

A single flash of light off a knife blade gave Slocum only a fraction of a second warning before the rope went slack and sent him tumbling back to the bottom of the pit.

Slocum landed hard on his back, gasped in pain to regain his breath and then fumbled for his six-gun. He cocked it and pointed upward, waiting for the owlhoot who had cut the rope to show himself. Slocum figured the man wanted to gloat. To do that properly, he had to look down at his handiwork.

But no grinning, leering face appeared for Slocum to take his shot. He had heard the man approaching but no sound accompanied his retreat. He had severed the rope to strand Slocum, then left right away.

Slocum waited another few minutes until it became obvious he wasn't going to get a shot. He had answered the question of why Mikhail had been dropped into the hole after he'd been killed. A lure. Bait. For someone incautious enough to go after the corpse rather than hunt for the killer first.

Taking an inventory of what he had disheartened Slocum. He had ten feet of rope cut off at the edge of the pit. A dozen or so matches, his six-shooter and whatever might be on Mikhail's body. Slocum swallowed his distaste for searching a corpse, only to find that Mikhail didn't have anything that would help him escape the pit. The great bear of a man didn't have his two pistols on him, but he might have dropped them on the far side of the opening above.

In disgust, Slocum sat back on his heels, then began a slow survey of his rocky prison. The walls were too far apart for him to brace his back against one side and his feet on the other so he could walk up the chimney to the cave floor above. If anything the six-foot-by-six-foot pit was like a too deep, too wide grave.

Slocum made a half dozen circuits of the cave before deciding the wall opposite the one he had come down was the most likely to afford him an escape route. Jagged rocks protruded on the wall. He would cut his hands to ribbons if he wasn't careful, but the fifteen-foot span of rock afforded his only route for climbing. Slocum took the length of rope, tied it into a loop, then knotted it several more times so he could hang onto it. Taking a deep breath, Slocum began climbing.

Fingers clung to small stones barely visible from below. What worried him more was finding secure ledges for his boots. Inching upward, Slocum got halfway up the wall before he felt the rocky ledges under his boots beginning to give way. Frantically, he looked around for a new step. He didn't see any.

He knew that he would never make it back, even this far, if he had to start over. Slocum swung the loop of rope up and over the edge of the pit. It slid back. A foot slipped, leaving him dangling by one foot and his left handhold. Slocum arched his back and tossed the rope again as his foothold broke free.

Slocum pitched down, then yelled in pain as his fall snapped to a stop only a couple feet lower. His rope had circled a rock on the cave floor. Slocum swung around by his right handgrip, glad now he had put in the extra knots. Releasing his left hand, he gripped the rope with both hands, spun around and got his feet against the wall.

The rope seemed to stretch ominously. Slocum realized the rock anchor above his head was coming free. Wasting no time, Slocum scrambled up, his feet slipping and scraping against the pit wall. Hand over hand got him to the edge of the hole as the rock pulled free of its moorings. Slocum got dirt in his face, but this only spurred him on. Feet driving hard, arms straining, he pulled himself up and over the rim of the pit to fall belly down on the cave floor.

He lay panting, then remembered how he had been stranded at the bottom of the abyss. Slocum rolled to the side, his bloodied hands going for his six-shooter. He got to his feet and stared into the complete darkness beyond the small circle lit from above.

The wind blowing into his face calmed him a mite. But try as he might, he couldn't see or hear anything of the lily-livered owlhoot who had tried to strand him in the hole.

Slocum dropped to one knee and examined the floor. From the mud-and-blood mixture, he guessed he had been right about how Mikhail had met his end. The Russian had vaulted the pit, only to find a knife rammed into his guts. Slocum made out the spot where Mikhail had lain until he died. The evidence of how he had been pushed into the pit was gone, thanks as much to Slocum's exit from the hole as anything else.

Edging around the area, using the light from above as his sole illumination, Slocum saw that Mikhail had not gone any farther than this spot. But the tracks in the dust on the cave floor became confusing. Without snow and rain coming from the hole in the roof—and Mikhail's blood—mud had not formed here. The thin dust didn't hold much in the way of tracks, but Slocum found definite signs someone had come and gone several times.

He didn't know if the man who had tried to maroon him had left the cave or had come back this way. Slocum followed his instincts and went deeper into the cave. For twenty feet the cave ran straight, the chimney in the roof affording some small illumination. Then the cave took an oblique turn to the right and plunged down sharply into the bowels of the earth.

Slocum hesitated to go farther without a torch or miner's lantern to show the way, but he was riled up over Mikhail's death and someone trying to strand him at the bottom of the pit with the dead Russian. Caution started to get the better of him when Slocum heard something moving in the dark.

He reached into his pocket, pulled out a lucifer and shifted it to his left hand. Taking his six-shooter firmly in his right, he struck the match.

The flare cast a sudden light that forced him to take in everything in a rush. Slocum blinked from the glare but saw a dozen paces deeper in the cave a deadly, long, thin-bladed knife held by . . . Elizabeth Bartlett.

The match sputtered out unexpectedly, leaving Slocum momentarily blind. He stepped back, waiting for the woman to attack.

8

For an instant Elizabeth stared at Slocum, the knife glinting wickedly in her hand. Then she let out a shriek, dropped the knife with a clatter and plunged into the darkness.

Slocum was as startled as the woman. He stood with the cold wall pressing against his left arm and the wind gusting from the depths of the cave. The ring of metal against rock faded quickly, leaving Slocum to wonder if he had imagined seeing Elizabeth at all. He pulled out another match and lit it.

The knife blade shone where the brunette had dropped it on the dusty cave floor. Slocum advanced as if it might spring up and stab him in the belly. He crouched down, laid his six-shooter where it would be close at hand should he need it, then gingerly picked up the knife. Slocum examined it near it the sputtering match flame and saw dark stains on the blade.

Blood stains.

It didn't take much of an imagination to believe Elizabeth had plunged this knife into Mikhail's belly, twisted it hard and killed him. That left a lot of questions unanswered, though. Had Mikhail cornered her by accident, thinking he had found the man who had tried to ambush him? Seeing a mountain of gristle and mean like Mikhail lumbering forward, growling like an enraged bear, could spook anyone. Elizabeth might have only defended herself against what she thought was a savage attack.

That didn't explain why she was in the cave. She had told Slocum she was hunting for her husband, Ned. Underground seemed a curious place to look for a wayward spouse. Slocum shook his head. Guessing got him nowhere. He needed answers.

Slocum tucked the knife into his belt, then considered what he ought to do. He couldn't continue burning his matches. There were fewer than a dozen left in their tin container.

"Elizabeth!" he called. "It's me, Slocum! You remember me? We found that line shack and . . ." Slocum let his words die out. The woman might have found her husband in this cave. Trying to explain to him why his wife and a drifter had spent the night together was more than Slocum wanted to tackle right now.

He listened as his words echoed away into the dark distance. No returning cry answered his. Tossed on the horns of a dilemma, Slocum wavered a few seconds, then came to a decision. He hadn't come this far to turn around and run back to Anastasia in her comfortable Goldust hotel room. What could he tell her other than Mikhail was dead?

More than this, Slocum had a score to settle. It looked as if Elizabeth might have not only stranded him purposefully at the bottom of the pit by cutting his climbing rope, she might also have murdered Mikhail. Slocum needed to know for sure.

Resolve firm now, he began unraveling his lariat and spinning the sturdy threads into a thin string. He worked furiously for close to a half hour, then looked at the pile of twine at his feet. He spent a few more minutes rolling it into a ball that he could easily carry. Slocum tied one end of the string around a rock, tugged gently to be sure it wouldn't come loose, then picked up the ball of hemp string and started into the darkness, unrolling it behind him.

He carefully checked the floor with every step. No amount of string would let him climb out of another pit. The total blackness quickly engulfed him, and the only guide he had was the strong breeze against his face. Slocum knew he might have used that to get out of the cave; all he had to do was keep it at his back. Then the wisdom of his plan made itself known. A Y branch, each with its own breeze, forced him to light another match to study the floor for a hint as to which path Elizabeth had taken.

One had been scuffed and the rock dust had been kicked around. The other showed no such traffic. By the time the match went out, Slocum was a dozen paces down the tunnel Elizabeth had taken.

He began to wonder how she maneuvered through the cave so quickly and surely without any light. Blundering about would have produced sounds Slocum had never heard. The only explanation was that Elizabeth Bartlett made her way through known territory. He added another question to the pile he had already accumulated. How had the woman become so familiar with the cave?

Slocum unrolled his string as he went, making sure it never got tangled. His progress was painfully slow, but Slocum knew the penalty for rushing. After what seemed an eternity of shuffling and unwinding, Slocum stopped and stared ahead. He thought his eyes were fooling him. Then he rubbed his eyes and focused on a tiny point of light bobbing along like a will-o'-the-wisp. He drew his six-shooter and started to let off a round just as the light vanished.

"Elizabeth?" he called. His voice was drowned out

quickly, the noisy rush of wind swallowing it. But he had seen light. Who else could be in the cave?

Slocum chanced another match, having to cup his hand over it when he realized how brisk the wind was coming up this tunnel. As it burned, he looked around quickly. A slow smile came to his lips when he saw a rock ledge in the tunnel ahead. On it lay a dozen or more miner's candles. Before his match died, Slocum rushed ahead and grabbed a stubby candle, applying the flame to the charred wick.

The candle guttered, then began burning with a pure, yellow light. Slocum was astounded at how much illumination the small candle cast. His eyes had adjusted to utter darkness, and now he had enough light to force him to squint. He stuffed a half dozen more candles in his pockets before turning back to face the wind.

He didn't see any trace of the dancing mote of light ahead in the tunnel. Elizabeth must have known the candles were stored on this ledge and had taken one, using it to guide herself deeper into the cave. Slocum continued unrolling the twine behind him. He guessed that more than two hundred feet stretched behind him. He couldn't go much farther unless he abandoned his method of finding his way back above ground.

"Elizabeth!" he called again. Slocum cocked his head and listened against the whistle of wind and heard a faint, feminine cry, followed by a sudden gasp.

He picked up the pace, cupping the flame with his hand. Now and then he had to fiddle with the ball of twine he was unrolling. Slocum was coming to the end of the rope he had so carefully refashioned. But Elizabeth held answers to all his questions.

Slocum stopped dead in his tracks and listened harder, thinking he heard movement behind him. He turned, held up the candle and looked into the tunnel he had just traversed. When he saw nothing, Slocum thought his nerves were beginning to wear thin. Finding Mikhail and then being trapped in the pit with the Russian's corpse had put him on edge.

The dark, the incessant wind and Elizabeth Bartlett holding the bloody knife had added to his unease.

Slocum unrolled more twine, then set out again in the direction of the faint sounds ahead. Now and then he stopped at crossing tunnels, but none of them showed signs of recent travel. Slocum dropped to his knees and carefully studied one that held old footprints, tracks slowly blown away by the wind down the main shaft. Someone else had entered and explored this labyrinth of tunnels, but not recently. From the size of the prints, it had not been Elizabeth.

When hot wax dribbled over his fingers, Slocum took another candle from his pocket and lit it from the old flame before it snuffed itself out. Hot tallow scent in his nostrils, he sucked in his breath, then set out after Elizabeth again.

This time he heard scurrying sounds like a rat in a barn. He unrolled more of his twine, then stopped when he stepped into a large cavern. The light from his guttering miner's candle failed to reach the top of the vault or the far end of the rocky chamber. The sides were less than ten yards in either direction, forming a long gallery like the inside of a church.

"Where are you, Elizabeth? I hear you, but I don't see you. I just want to talk." Slocum wasn't sure that was entirely true. If she had murdered Mikhail, she would likely try to kill him, too. But Slocum wanted to know why.

"Go away. You don't know what you're getting into."

Slocum homed in on the sound of the woman's petulant voice. Her tone didn't match her furtive behavior. He took a few steps, then came to the end of his rope. Slocum dropped the end of his twine, glad that it had brought him this far. He decided there wouldn't be any problem locating the tunnel where the string lay since it was the only opening behind him. Holding his candle high above his head with his left hand, he rested his right on the butt of his six-gun.

"What's going on? Why are you in the cave?" He started to ask the woman if she had killed Mikhail, then remembered he had not found the Russian's two pistols. Elizabeth might have both of them trained on him as he blundered through the cavern.

"You'll get us both killed," Elizabeth said. She stood, showing herself from behind a pale white, rounded stalagmite a few yards ahead. She reached down and put a miner's candle on the rock beside her so the dancing light cast eerie shadows across her face. Slocum couldn't read her expression.

"What happened to Mikhail? The Russian?"

"I don't want to talk about that," Elizabeth said.

"Have you found your husband? Is he hiding out in these caves?"

"You ask too damn many questions," she said angrily. The brunette tossed her head back to get the hair from her wild eyes, but the wind blowing through the cavern caught it and dropped it back over her face.

"Why'd you try to strand me in the pit?" Slocum asked. A steely edge came to his voice now. He was tired of trying to coax Elizabeth to give him what he wanted to know.

"You'll ruin everything," she said. With more fear than before, she added, "We'll both die if you don't leave now."

Slocum started to speak but was cut off by the woman's shrill scream. His six-shooter came from its holster, and he had it aimed in her direction before he realized she was reacting to something behind him. Slocum took a step forward, spun and went into a crouch. The quick spin caused the candle to gutter and cast shadows in all the wrong places.

"Hands up!" Slocum called, seeing a dim shape dart from rock to rock in the direction of the entrance.

He started to fire but was blinded by the muzzle flash as his stalker shot first. Slocum heard lead whine past his head. He dived for cover, losing his candle as he hit the rocky floor and rolled behind a small rock patterned like a water-stained map. He poked his head around, hunting for a target.

Along with his candle flame, the shadows disappeared soundlessly. He heard soft sounds of boots scuffing along the dusty floor. Otherwise, he had no proof anyone else was even in the cave.

"Are you all right, Elizabeth?" he called. At the moment he didn't care if she had dropped into a crevice all the way to the fires of hell. He hoped she would answer and distract the gunman who had tried to ventilate him. Slocum's ploy didn't work. Neither Elizabeth nor the backshooter responded in any way.

Sidling along, Slocum wended his way through the forest of rocks poking their way up off the floor. The rocks were as dry as a bone, and few were more than waist high. The only guide he had in the pitch black was the wind blowing endlessly from the far end of the gallery.

When he had gone a dozen yards, Slocum saw the faint glow from Elizabeth's candle. She hunched over it, trying to hide the light without putting out the flame.

She looked up, eyes wide with fright when he came up on her.

"Time to tell me what's going on," he said.

"This isn't any of your business, Slocum," she said harshly.

"I got men shooting at my back, Mikhail got knifed in the belly, I was almost trapped in a pit with his body and you're telling me none of it's my business? You're wrong."

"We need to get away. Then we can talk."

Slocum looked around and saw nothing but deep black in the cave.

"Where do we go?"

"I . . . I don't know. I got so turned around when you started chasing me, I don't know where I am. Can you get out?"

Slocum wondered if she were lying. He thought so, but getting out the windy cave and having the wan winter sun shining on his face again struck him as the best idea he'd had the livelong day.

"You follow me. I can find the way back to the surface with no problem."

Elizabeth let out a sigh of relief that sounded genuine. Slocum had to wonder what the hell was going on.

Drifting like a shadow, he made his way back toward the tunnel leading into the cavern. Now and then he stopped to listen but heard nothing of the backshooter.

"I think we're alone," Slocum said. "I don't hear anything but the wind."

"The damn wind," muttered Elizabeth. "Gets on my nerves something fierce."

Slocum reached to take the candle from her hand. Elizabeth recoiled as if he had tried to rape her.

"No!" she said.

"Then you go straight ahead and find the tunnel. I'll follow you."

Elizabeth thought about it for a moment, and to Slocum's surprise stood up and walked slowly ahead. Her fear of losing the candle outweighed the chance she might be cut down by a hail of bullets.

She hadn't gone five feet when she called back to him, "How'd you mark your trail?"

"I unrolled a ball of twine," he said, seeing no reason not to tell her.

"No!" she shrieked, running forward. *"No!"*

He matched her pace, then dashed past her when he saw what she already had. A tiny river of fire flowed toward them as the twine burned from the other end.

9

Slocum watched the twine burn swiftly like a miner's fuse. Then it sizzled and went out a few feet in front of him. Slocum heard Elizabeth crying in anguish behind him, but he ignored the woman. Someone had set fire to the carefully laid twine that would have led him out of the cave safely and quickly. He drew his six-shooter and started into the tunnels, hunting for someone to shoot.

"Wait, Slocum, don't let them ambush you!" cried Elizabeth Bartlett. The brunette grabbed for his arm to pull him back, but Slocum shrugged her off. He was in no mood to hide. He had been shot at and had people killed all around him. Now someone wanted to maroon him in the depths of a winding, twisty system of confusing caves. He was fed up and madder than a wet hen.

Somebody had to pay.

"Show yourselves!" Slocum shouted. His words echoed along the tunnels and were quickly drowned out by the constant wind blowing at his back. Stepping into the narrower tunnel from the huge cavern caused the wind to blow harder at his back.

Slocum wasn't as upset over losing his twine safety line as he might have been. All he needed to do to get out of the cave was to keep the wind at his back. But nobody got away with sniping at him and acting the coward trying to maroon him like this.

"Slocum, no, no," whimpered Elizabeth. He kept walking, the thin trail of ash showing where the twine had burned thoroughly. Slocum stopped now and then and listened hard.

Nothing but the cool breeze filled his ears, a ghostly presence whispering sweet nothings to him. Then he put down the candle and pressed his left hand against the rocky wall. He waited for a few seconds, then smiled. Vibration from running feet came through the rock, telling him he wasn't on the trail of a spook.

"You don't know what's going on," Elizabeth said fearfully.

"What are you down here for?" Slocum asked.

"My husband. Ned. I'm looking for Ned." Elizabeth was almost out of breath now, gasping in reaction to all that had happened.

"Maybe it's your husband who set fire to my string," Slocum said.

"He—no, it wasn't Ned."

"I'm going to find out. Stay here." Slocum picked up the candle and headed down the tunnel, sure that someone ran ahead of him by the way the footfalls caused vibration along the walls.

"Don't leave me, please."

Slocum was past caring what the woman did or didn't do. He pushed on. Elizabeth waited a few seconds, then dashed after him. He wasn't sure if he was pleased to have her with him. It made tracking the owlhoot in the caves more difficult, but Slocum had questions for her that she had yet to answer.

"Hold this," Slocum said, shoving the sputtering miner's candle into her hands. He wanted to keep one hand on the wall and the other on his pistol.

"They can see us."

"And if we put out the candle, we can't see them," Slocum said, disgusted with her. She knew who was ahead in the tunnel and wasn't telling. His long strides followed the ashen path until he came to the Y in the tunnels. Or was it the one he remembered? Slocum studied the intersection and frowned at what he found—or didn't find.

The charred path of twine ended here.

"What is it?" asked Elizabeth, anxiously looking around.

"They cut the twine here and rolled it back up. From this spot on, they set fire to it," Slocum guessed. "That tunnel leads out." He pointed to the one on his right but looked skeptically at the branching tunnel. Wind gusted out of it, also, but he felt the faint footsteps down there. "Go on. Get to the surface and wait for me." Slocum was a little reluctant to tell Elizabeth to go since she was likely to steal his horse and leave him stranded.

"That's not the way out," she said. "I'm sure of it. This is." She stepped into the tunnel Slocum had intended entering to pursue the firebug who had set fire to his twine.

"No, it's not. This goes deeper into the cave." Then something else struck Slocum. If the twine leading to the surface had been rolled up from here so it wouldn't leave an ash trail and somebody was ahead of them in the branching tunnel, that meant at least two men were rambling around in the caves. No matter which way Slocum went, he would have one man ahead and another behind him.

It wouldn't be pretty getting trapped between two gunmen in a tunnel. His only option was to retreat to the large cavern, but what would he do there?

"Where does the large cave lead? The one where I found you."

"I don't know," Elizabeth said, and he knew she was

lying. Seeing his reaction, she hurriedly added, "Ned's not that way, so I didn't go too far. More tunnels lead off. A half dozen or so, but no one had walked down them recently."

Slocum wasn't sure he could believe a word she said. Elizabeth had her own concerns and the more she talked, the less he thought they had anything to do with him.

"That way," Slocum said, coming to a decision. He started into the branching tunnel, the wind in his face. He had hunted enough to know the advantage of scent to a predator. Wolves and coyotes always circled downwind and then stalked their prey by going upwind. This way not only was their own scent blown away from the prey, any small sounds would also go along with the wind.

Slocum hoped this small advantage worked to his benefit as he hiked down the narrow tunnel. Here and there the walls crimped down, forcing him to turn sideways and force himself through. This convinced him Elizabeth either had not known or had lied about this being the way out. Slocum hadn't passed any narrowing of the walls on his way to the large cavern.

He noticed the woman didn't desert him but pressed close, clutching the candle as if it were her lifeline. Slocum motioned for her to stay put so he could walk a few yards farther along the tunnel to get away from the heavy wax scent from the candle. He sucked in a deep breath and let his nose work. The lack of mustiness in the wind made him wonder about the caves and if any animals had dens inside. He doubted it. That made the acrid scent he picked up all the more important.

"Ahead," he said softly to Elizabeth. "Not too far, either. At least one man who doesn't bother taking baths regularly. How's that square with your husband's habits?"

"I . . . I don't know. He might have been in this maze for weeks."

Slocum wanted to ask why she thought that, but he had

other matters to tend to first. He pressed his hand against
the wall and felt faint vibrations. Slocum held up his hand
and silently ordered Elizabeth to stay put.

He had a job to do. Slocum hadn't gone a dozen paces
when the light from the candle faded to nothing. He let
his eyes adjust to the dark and stared ahead, trying to pick
out any light from ahead. The man he pursued had to have
some way of illuminating his way through the twisty,
turny rabbit warren.

Slocum walked steadily, his nose working like a blood-
hound's. The body odor from the man ahead faded as the
wind gusted unexpectedly hard. Slocum hurried ahead to
catch up and found a narrowing in the tunnel where the
wind blew past like a small tornado.

He wedged himself between the rocks and popped out
on the far side in almost total darkness. Operating by hearing and scent, he turned slowly, hunting for his quarry.

For a minute he swiveled back and forth, his Colt Navy
ready to fire. When he realized he got no feeling of anyone near, he backed up, got through the constriction in
the tunnel and saw Elizabeth right away. She had come
after him.

"I told you to wait," Slocum said angrily.

"The candle's burning out. Look." She held out a shaky
hand and showed him only a dime-thin layer of tallow
remained around the burning wick.

Slocum fumbled in his pocket and found another candle, lighting it off the dying one.

"Come on," Slocum said, going back to where he had
lost the trail. This time he had enough light to see what
had happened. Four tunnels lead away, making the juncture something of a major intersection in the tangle of
tunnels. Slocum heaved a sigh and set to work finding
where the man had gone. To his disgust all the tunnel
floors showed recent scuff marks. He might as well have

been outside the busiest sporting club in Denver for all the traffic that had passed through here.

"We'll go into the wind," Slocum decided. Then he noticed that all the tunnels were gusting wind. He tried to figure how this was possible, then realized leaving the caverns by keeping the wind to his back wasn't going to be as easy as it had seemed. Even the tunnel he had taken into the juncture puffed and wheezed a little, showing wind from other points were making the simple expedient impossible.

"There's no wind deeper in the caves," Elizabeth said. "We should stay here and try to find our way out."

"I thought you wanted to find your husband."

"I want to stay alive. We're both going to die down here, Slocum. I know it!" A touch of hysteria entered her voice again.

Slocum turned slowly, examining the walls and even the roofs of the tunnels for any trace of recent passage. He kept returning to the tunnel directly in front of the one he had used to reach this point. Nothing distinguished it from the others, but Slocum obeyed his gut and started down it.

"Come on," he said when he stepped into inky black because Elizabeth hung back with the candle.

"No, don't do this. We can go back. We know there has to be another way out. The other tunnel! We can—"

"Go on, then," Slocum said harshly. If Elizabeth left him he could always light one of the candles he had stashed in his pocket. He had matches and he had the determination to put an end to the backshooting. As he reached down to his coat pocket, his hand brushed the cold hilt of the knife he had picked up after Elizabeth had dropped it.

"Did you kill Mikhail? The Russian?" he asked bluntly. Slocum had hoped the quick change of topic would catch the woman off guard.

"What difference does it make if you lead us both to our deaths?"

"You already tried to kill me," Slocum said, turning toward her and lifting his six-gun. "What reason can you give me not to gun you down?"

"I'm a woman! You can't."

"You cut the rope, stranding me in the pit."

"I . . . I was frightened. I didn't know it was you."

"Who'd you think it was? Your husband?"

"No!" cried Elizabeth. "I don't want to hurt him."

Slocum heard more than the simple truth in that, but what more he wasn't going to take the time to ferret out. From behind, deeper in the cave, he heard the telltale scratching sounds of boots moving across the rock dust on the floor. He lifted his forefinger to his lips to silence Elizabeth, then spun and hurried toward the sound.

He didn't catch the sour sweat smell on the wind this time. But the sound grew louder as he made his way along the stony corridor. The tunnel narrowed and widened a few more times, but Elizabeth kept up with him and didn't bother yammering about her innocence. Slocum had gotten her to confess to cutting his rope. He needed to find out if she had also killed Mikhail. He thought she had.

The "who" was being answered but the "why" for her crimes eluded Slocum at the moment. He decided there would be a better time to interrogate Elizabeth.

A dancing mote of light that shone brightly and then disappeared sporadically alerted him that he had overtaken his quarry. He stepped in front of Elizabeth to shield some of the light from their candle. The rays still lit up the tunnel, though possibly not so brightly as to be noticed by someone carrying a lantern.

"He's ahead and coming toward us," Slocum said. He steered Elizabeth toward a niche in the rock, pushed her in and then crowded behind her. He jerked when he felt heat on his hand and knew she had shoved the candle flame against him. He bit back a curse as the man in the tunnel hurried past.

Slocum let him get a few feet farther, then slipped out and trained his six-gun at the man's back.

"Hands up or I'll drill you," Slocum commanded coldly.

The man jumped in surprise and started to turn.

"Freeze," Slocum warned. "Keep those hands where I can see them."

"I don't know what this is about," the man said, looking over his shoulder.

"The hell you don't," Slocum said, getting angrier by the second. He was tired of everyone pretending to be babes in the wood and to know nothing.

Elizabeth worked her way from the rocky nook and stood beside him. From the corner of his eye, Slocum saw the brunette stiffen. She stepped forward a pace and thrust the candle in front of her to better illuminate their prisoner.

"You!" she cried.

The man whirled, eyes wide, and faced them. He ignored Slocum and the threat posed by his leveled six-shooter as he stared at the woman in the light cast by his small lantern.

"Elizabeth!"

"Don't tell me," Slocum said, anger fading and replaced by resignation to his strange fate.

"John Slocum," said the woman, "meet my husband, Ned Bartlett."

10

"Who're you?" demanded Ned Bartlett of Slocum.

"I'm the one holding the six-gun," Slocum said, his anger returning. He had been shot at and marooned and run pillar to post and was in no mood to answer questions. "What are you doing in this cave?"

Bartlett blinked. His mouth opened and then snapped shut. Determination settled on him like a blanket, and Slocum saw that getting anything from the man would take more than asking a question or two.

"Why'd you leave me?" asked Elizabeth, pushing past Slocum. The candle bobbed about in her hand. As she stabbed a finger out to poke into her husband's chest, hot wax spilled. Bartlett recoiled, as much from the wax as the prodding. "You lit out and never let me know where you were going. I had to track you down."

"He's not working for you?" Bartlett looked suspiciously at Slocum.

"He's just some cowboy who happened along," Elizabeth said. The two ignored Slocum and his six-shooter, so he holstered it and reached into his pocket to pull out another candle. Bartlett held a small miner's lantern, and the candle Elizabeth waved around provided a fair amount

93

of light but the two were slowly inching away from him. Slocum wanted to keep the upper hand. For that he needed to be able to see.

"You just picked him up and brought him down here? How could you be so downright dumb?" shouted Bartlett. This got him a hard slap across the face. He looked startled, then reared back to punch Elizabeth with his fist.

He froze when he realized Slocum was pushing back his duster to get his Colt Navy out again. The expression on Slocum's face told the man hitting a woman, even one who had slapped him, wasn't going to go unpunished.

"I'm sorry, Beth," Bartlett said. "It's just that there's so much at stake. I ain't sharin' with nobody, much less some drifter who's been—" Bartlett bit off the rest of his sentence when he saw both Slocum's and Elizabeth's expressions.

"Why are you prowling around down here?" Slocum asked. "That's not a casual question you can dodge. You've got five seconds to think about telling me the truth." Slocum spun on Elizabeth and said, "You! Keep quiet."

"But—" Elizabeth fell silent when she saw how determined Slocum was. "Go on, Ned. Tell him. He won't let us be until he finds out everything. He's that way."

"Yeah," Slocum said. "I'm that way." He watched closely to see if Ned Bartlett was going to lie to him. Slocum couldn't tell because of the play of emotions on the man's face. Seeing his estranged wife had upset his applecart something fierce.

"Look around," Bartlett said. "Caves. Miles and miles of natural caves. And what's been found in 'bout every stream around here? Gold! I reckoned that there were plenty of veins of gold—maybe even the mother lode!— waiting to be found."

Ned Bartlett didn't have the look of a prospector. Slocum had seen the man's like before and usually there were wanted posters chasing after him. He was more inclined to steal a nickel than he was to work for an honest dollar.

"If the gold's found in streams, that means it's washed down from higher on the mountain," Slocum pointed out.

"But there are other mines," Bartlett rushed to tell him. "Why kill myself shovelin' a ton or two of dirt to find a couple ounces of gold when the mines are already dug?"

"I didn't see much evidence that any of the mines in this part of the countryside were successful. Most of the strikes are on the far side of Goldust."

"That's the beauty of my scheme," Bartlett said. "Let them hunt somewhere else. I'll find a vein of gold so thick I can use a knife to dig out nuggets. And I won't have to blast or cart out all that dross."

"He's a genius, my husband is," Elizabeth said in a neutral voice.

Slocum thought she was taking a dig at Bartlett, but he couldn't tell. The notion of finding gold in the meandering caves didn't seem too likely. Slocum was no expert, but the rock all around them wasn't the kind where gold was ever found. The caves were dry, and even animals avoided them.

"You see any trace of Indians while you've been exploring?" Slocum asked.

"Indians? Why, no, no trace of anyone else down here. It's like I'm the first man to hunt for gold here."

Slocum mulled over that. The Indians might think the Earth Spirit's breath was sacred and avoided the caves, or it could be any of a number of other things. There was no telling what would spook a Sioux or Blackfoot. The Indians weren't inclined to go out of their way to find gold like the white man—that set the stage for any number of battles over the land. Slocum hated to admit it, but Bartlett might have come up with a decent idea.

Still, the rocks looked wrong.

"How much gold have you found? Any quartz?" Slocum's eyes narrowed when he saw all that Bartlett carried with him was the tin lantern. Even a lazy prospector would have a pick to knock off an outcropping or two to see if the gold lurked beneath its crust.

"I—no," Bartlett said.

"He's not much of a miner," Elizabeth chimed in. "For all that, he's not much of a husband, either."

Slocum couldn't help reflecting on how different her attitude was now compared to when she had tried to enlist his aid to find Ned Bartlett. Then she had been the grieving wife, and now she was the shrew.

"You can't say that," Bartlett snapped. Elizabeth turned and whispered furiously. Bartlett got red in the face with anger and replied, but too low for Slocum to overhear. He decided to let the two argue a while and see if anything came from it. One thing they had both said that he took as the gospel truth. They were married. From the way they stood and argued, they were definitely married.

Slocum tried to figure out what had happened between them. After a few minutes of watching Ned Bartlett, he figured that the man had left his wife and come up here on a wild goose chase. Whether it had anything to do with finding gold in dry caves under the Dakota Black Hills was another matter. The man's search was more important than the marriage, though. Slocum made that out quite clearly. Elizabeth wasn't as upset over him leaving her as she was that he had dealt her out of whatever scheme brought him to this country.

"Enough!" Slocum shouted. "Stop your fighting. I'm sick of listening to you and want some straight answers."

"What is it?" demanded Elizabeth petulantly.

"Which of you killed Mikhail? The big Russian?"

Ned Bartlett looked as if he were the one getting the knife shoved into his guts. He started to speak, but Elizabeth cut him off.

"The Russian attacked me. He surprised me while I was

looking for Ned, and I just . . . reacted. I didn't mean to kill him."

"Did he attack you or did he startle you?" Slocum saw his question was going unanswered. "Why did you cut the rope to strand me at the bottom of the pit?"

"I didn't know who you were. It was dark. What if you'd been a friend of that Russian fellow?" protested Elizabeth. Slocum knew a lie when he heard it. She had probably killed Mikhail and had then had sliced the rope to leave Slocum to die at the bottom of the pit alongside the Russian.

Bartlett looked at his wife, but it wasn't in horror at the idea she had killed one man and had tried to murder another. There was a touch of admiration in his gaze. This sealed Slocum's opinion of the pair. They were lowdown sneak thieves and killers.

"We're getting out of these caves right now," Slocum said. "Since you burned the twine I left to mark the path, you'll have to lead us out."

"What twine?" asked Bartlett. He looked at his wife. Slocum and Elizabeth stiffened in reaction when it became obvious that Bartlett had nothing to do with burning the twine.

"Who else is down here?" asked Slocum. "You have any partners?"

"Nobody," Bartlett said, trying and failing to look innocent. He quickly added, "Except for Beth, that is."

"You lying sack of shit," the woman snarled. "You would have cut me out entirely. It's a good thing I found you before you got to the—" Elizabeth's words were cut off when Bartlett clamped his hand over her mouth to keep her from spilling the beans.

Slocum was past caring what they were searching for underground. The low ceilings and tight passages had begun to wear on his nerves. While there wasn't the incessant wind blowing through this section of the caves, it made him edgy knowing he had to face it again before winning free to the surface. Most of all he wanted to see the winter sun high overhead in a brilliant blue Dakota sky.

"Lead the way out of here," Slocum ordered. "You know the way. You've been 'exploring' underground long enough to know, don't you?" He stared hard at Bartlett, who withered under his steely gaze. The man averted his eyes and murmured something Slocum didn't catch.

"You're a scoundrel, Ned Bartlett," his wife raged. She shoved him back down the tunnel she and Slocum had used to find the man. Bartlett started walking, his lantern bobbing about. Elizabeth walked close behind, castigating him for all manner of things. Slocum listened with half an ear. Their domestic problems were less of a concern to him than their obviously illegal ones.

One of them had killed Mikhail. If Slocum had to guess, his money rode on Elizabeth Bartlett. She had also tried to leave him in the pit with the dead Russian. It was possible Elizabeth was covering for her husband, but it didn't seem all that likely. Slocum wondered how a real fight between the murdering woman and her milk-toast husband would come out. Ned Bartlett obviously found hightailing it away from Elizabeth better than confronting her.

They walked a few minutes, the darkness in the tunnel closing in as their candles burned lower and lower. Slocum kept the pair in sight but when they came to a narrowing, he had to twist sideways and wiggle hard to get through. When he popped out on the far side, they were nowhere to be seen.

"Bartlett!" Slocum bellowed. "Don't think you can hide from me!" Slocum hurried down the tunnel and came to a juncture he didn't remember seeing. The sudden gust of wind from deeper in the cave blew out his candle. Rather than try to relight it, Slocum stood stock-still for a moment and let his eyes adjust to the utter darkness. Then he tried to find any sign of the Bartletts.

Whichever way they had gone, they hid their light well. He saw nothing and heard only the wind.

"Don't try to hide. I'll root you out!" Slocum shouted. The words echoed down the branching tunnels and finally died. He failed to flush them from their hiding place. Slocum pressed his hand against a rocky wall and waited. No vibration. This pretty well confirmed his guess that they had gone to ground somewhere, hiding in a rocky cranny waiting for their chance.

Bartlett hadn't been packing iron that Slocum saw, but that didn't mean the man didn't have a pistol or even a rifle hidden away somewhere in the maze of tunnels. If Elizabeth had been armed with anything more than the knife Slocum had taken from her, she would have used it before now. The more Slocum thought on it, the luckier he was that he had kept her ahead of him in the tunnels. Without a gun or knife, she was likely to have found a rock and crowned him with it.

Slocum waited a few more minutes before deciding the two were either so far away in the caverns he would never locate them or they were accustomed to playing a waiting game. Turning slowly, he found the strongest gust of wind coming from a tunnel, then spun in a quick about-face and walked forward. He bounced off a rocky wall, felt carefully and found a new tunnel. With the wind at his back he kept walking.

When he had gone a dozen paces, he stopped to relight his miner's candle. Stepping into a pit that would swallow him up forever was the last thing Slocum wanted. With his body blocking the steady breeze, he walked forward, twice more going through junctures and having to make decisions as to the way out. The wind at his back helped but grew confusing at several places.

As suddenly as the sun coming out from behind a

cloud, Slocum stepped into the snowy Dakota landscape. He blinked at the glare and looked around. He had emerged from yet another of the caves, confirming his belief all the gusty mouths were connected underground.

He heaved a sigh of relief at getting free of the tunnels that were too much like a stony coffin for comfort, then hiked to the top of the hill and spotted his horse fitfully grazing a quarter mile off. At least he had a way back to Goldust to tell the duchess about Mikhail's untimely death.

11

Slocum tugged at the collar of his duster when the wind kicked up, again bitingly cold as the sun dipped below the horizon. He tried to keep a steady course back to Goldust but got lost twice, the snowy hills looking too similar for him to distinguish in the twilight. By the time the sun set and darkness almost as intense as that within the caves descended on him, he was frustrated and ready to keep riding, no matter the direction, until he came to somewhere else.

Anywhere else.

Only his duty to report Mikhail's death kept him from doing just that. Anastasia needed to know that her servant had died. What Slocum would tell her as to why Mikhail had been murdered swirled around in his head like the wind-driven motes of snow in front of his eyes. Elizabeth Bartlett had killed Mikhail. The reason was as clear as his path through the stormy night.

When the snowflakes began working their way under his duster and chilling him to the bone, Slocum knew he had to find a place to camp for the night. Not being too sure where he was made it harder to hunt for a line shack or abandoned mining cabin. He tried to figure out what direction he rode by waiting for clouds to part and give a clear view of the sky. Only a few seconds of staring upward told him he wasn't going to see the sky anytime soon. He had been lucky when he had emerged from the underground warren of caves to see blue, but he had wandered about lost longer than he had thought.

Right now he wished he could find one of those devil's mouths spewing forth a breath warmer than the freezing nighttime Dakota air. It had saved him once and might again. But where would he stumble across one? The snow grew thicker around him, forcing him to admit he had to make camp here and now or be so turned around he might never get back to Goldust.

He almost rode into a sheer rocky cliff rising from the land. Guiding his weary horse along the face, he found a crevice that widened quickly into a small box canyon. Without hesitation, Slocum led his horse through and into this protected area. The Black Hills were filled with surprises. This one happened to be one good enough to save his life.

Finding a spot to camp along a wall, Slocum scrounged dried wood and built a large fire for him and his horse. The animal had little enough to graze on unless it broke through the crusty ice covering the ground, but Slocum had brought enough trail rations for a hearty meal. He even opened a can of peaches in way of celebration. He had escaped the caves.

Slocum left his horse saddled. The saddle and blanket would provide a small measure of protection against the cold. He pulled his bedroll up around his shoulders and lay down by the fire, watching orange and yellow flames leap and cavort about hypnotically. All that had happened to him became a jumble as he tried to sort it out.

Elizabeth Bartlett had killed Mikhail and had tried to kill him. But who had shot at the hulking Russian giant back at the deserted mining camp? That hadn't been Elizabeth. When Slocum came across her so unexpectedly in the cave, she had carried only the bloody knife. She had tried to maroon him, too, but others were in the cave besides her husband. Someone had set fire to the twine Slocum had left to mark his way out and Ned Bartlett hadn't been responsible.

How many people roamed through those underground passages?

The mouth to hell. The devil's own mouth. Grinning. Gaping. Swallowing damned souls. That kept rolling over and over in Slocum's mind as he drifted off to a fitful sleep.

It took Slocum two days to find his way back to Goldust, and then he got lucky, finding the muddy road when a stagecoach came rattling through, its mules straining mightily and protesting even more. The thick, threatening clouds swept along low in the sky, blotting out direction, and with a uniform blanket of snow on the ground, Slocum would have been hard-pressed to find any landmark.

He rode to the side of the highway to keep his horse from stepping into a mudhole and breaking a leg. By his watch, he reached Goldust around noon on the third day after escaping the underground caves. He went directly to the hotel, wondering if Anastasia would be waiting or if she had moved on. For all her talk of devotion to her servant, Slocum wasn't sure the Russian duchess would let moss grow on her waiting to learn of Mikhail's fate.

Or his.

Slocum wearily dismounted and went into the hotel lobby, expecting a new round of strife with the room clerk. But the man looked up, his eyes went wide and he called to Slocum, "Wait right here, sir, while I fetch the duchess!" With that, the clerk hurried around the counter and took the stairs to the second floor three at a time.

Slocum sank into a chair at a card table on the far side

of the lobby, still not sure how he would break the news of Mikhail's death to her.

He was startled when he looked up and saw Anastasia standing next to his chair. He hadn't heard her approach.

"He's dead, isn't he?" the dark-haired duchess said flatly. "How did he die?"

"On the tip of this," Slocum said, drawing the knife Elizabeth had used and throwing it on the table. "I couldn't find out what happened, not exactly, but a woman named Elizabeth Bartlett probably killed him."

"A woman? Mikhail's carousing finally got the better of him? But he went after an ambusher. I do not understand."

"Elizabeth killed him in one of the caves and dumped him down into a pit. He might have startled her or she might have lain in wait for him. I caught her, then lost her and her husband in those damned caves."

"Gold," Anastasia muttered, almost under her breath.

"What's that? You know about the Bartletts hunting for gold in the caves? There's more than the pair of them looking," Slocum said. He felt as if he were running a race and everyone else was a mile ahead.

"Of course there is," Anastasia said. "Poor Mikhail. He should have never gone off on his own. Listening to you might have saved his life."

Slocum felt lucky rather than skillful at having avoided a similar fate in the caverns. The time had come for him to take matters into his own hands and act rather than react.

"There's no marshal in this town. That means whatever justice is to be done has to be done by me."

"By us, John," Anastasia said quietly. "Mikhail was a loyal servant. He deserves to be given a decent burial. Can you take me to the spot where I can retrieve his body? You need not do anything more."

"I need to do a powerful lot more," Slocum said, resolve hardening. "I want to see Elizabeth Bartlett in prison for killing Mikhail and maybe dangling at the end of a rope if she's done any more. And there's a good chance that she has."

"More?"

"Trying to kill me is one thing, but she might have thrown in with the men who murdered Scoggins."

"You have a one-track mind," Anastasia said, smiling slightly. "We shall see justice done, you and I together."

"There's no need for you to do anything else," Slocum said, willing to see this through to the end by himself. "Unless—"

"Unless what?" Anastasia stared at him, her ebony eyes unreadable. Slocum had hoped to get her to tell him more of her search in this godforsaken country. She hadn't come to the Dakotas on a lark. The Russian duchess had some end in mind and wasn't sharing it with him.

"Nothing. When can you be ready to go fetch Mikhail?"

"In one hour. I'll round up the rest of my servants, get a wagon loaded with supplies adequate for the task and meet you at the livery."

Slocum tried not to look surprised when Anastasia mentioned that she had more servants. He had seen only Mikhail and hadn't considered the possibility she had come from Russia with an entourage. This showed how little he knew of Russian royalty, or any royalty, for all that.

Anastasia put her hand on his, squeezed lightly, then hurried out the front door of the hotel to round up the rest of her attendants. Slocum wondered for a moment what chores she might have set them to in Goldust, then pushed it from his mind. He had to see that his mare got fed a proper nose bag of grain and groomed.

"And matches," Slocum said to himself. He wanted to be sure he had plenty of lucifers and maybe a fancy lantern like Ned Bartlett had before going back into the caves, even a little way.

Slocum grew madder by the minute, and it was at himself.

"I'm sorry, Anastasia, but I don't know where the cave is. I thought I could ride straight back to it, but the new snow covered my tracks."

"There is one good thing," Anastasia said morosely. "Mikhail will not spoil in such chilly weather." Even for the Russian duchess, the wind held a cutting edge that forced her to keep her greatcoat securely closed and a scarf pulled up to protect her lovely face.

"He's not likely to be eaten by wolves, either," Slocum said with the same gallows humor. "Not at the bottom of that pit."

The heavy clouds moved restlessly, changing their shadow patterns on the ground and further confusing him. What looked like a shallow depression one instant changed into a hill the next. The storm that had obliterated his tracks the night before had forced them to remain in their camp until almost noon.

Slocum glanced back and saw the light supply wagon struggling over the icy terrain. Three servants rode in it, two more on horseback. The three who kept the wagon moving had the look of servants, but the two riders were cut more from the cloth of a soldier. Cossacks, Anastasia had called them. Beneath their heavy beards glared unsmiling faces scarred repeatedly by knives or swords. In any fight Slocum would prefer them to be on his side.

He wondered where they had been up until now.

"Those hills look familiar," Slocum said. "If that craggy spire is the one I sighted in on when I was first going after Mikhail, the cave mouth ought to be less than a mile away."

"We should ride quickly," Anastasia said, glancing at the clouds. "A new storm is rumbling down out of Canada." She pushed away her scarf and sniffed at the wind. "It carries the scent of a true storm. Perhaps it blows from Russia!"

"I don't need another storm dumping a foot of snow on my head," Slocum said. He had survived some fierce storms in his day, but the endless train of them coming from the north had begun to make him yearn for soft, brown-skinned beauties in Mexico where it was warm and the tequila was the only fierce thing.

"You are impatient. I understand how you feel, John," she said, riding close to him and speaking so only he could hear. The Cossacks hung back a respectful distance. "There is no dishonor in losing the cave. There are so many."

"Not all of them snort the warm air."

"Warm feeling, yes," she said. "The air is held under the earth long enough to warm in the winter to the temperature of a pleasant autumn day. In the summer it is cooled to the same temperature. Winter, summer, it does not matter. The wind from below is a savior."

"You seem to know a lot about it," Slocum said.

"I have come across similar geologic formations," she said.

Before he could press her for more on her odd bits of knowledge, he reined back and stared. Then he smiled and pointed.

"Ahead. There's the cave. I'd bet money on it."

"Excellent," she said. "However, the wagon has become mired again." Anastasia rattled off a long series of commands in Russian to the Cossacks. "They will get the wagon to the cave. Let us go ahead."

Slocum knew there wasn't any danger. Elizabeth and Ned Bartlett would be long gone, but what of the unknown others who frequented the caverns? He dismissed his worry about them. Whatever they all searched for was not going to be found a few yards inside and at the bottom of a deep, rocky pit.

Anastasia rode ahead of him on her huge black stallion and stopped in front of the cave mouth. The horse turned tight circles and reared a little before she expertly controlled it.

"Something spooks my horse," she said as he trotted up. "Perhaps it smells death from inside."

Slocum hesitated a moment, staring at the rocky opening. Something didn't seem right to him, but he couldn't put a name to it. He opened his heavy duster and made certain he could reach his six-shooter, should the need arise. Then he fished about in his supplies for the miner's lantern.

"Will we need this?" Anastasia asked. "You said the pit was not far inside."

"It's far enough," Slocum said, having had his fill of blundering about in pitch black. He lit the candle and put it into the small box, opened the shutter enough to send the light out in a beam and then started into the cave.

Every step he took built the feeling that something was wrong.

About the point where he should have found the pit with Mikhail's body he stopped in disgust, realizing he had entered the wrong cave. Most of them looked similar on the surface. He had the misfortune of finding one that was more like the one where Mikhail had died than the others. Telling Anastasia would make him look like a fool in her eyes, but there wasn't any way around it.

As the duchess came into the cave, he turned to face her and held the lantern high.

"Anastasia, there's no need for you to come any farther," he called.

"I am no hothouse flower, John. I have seen dead men before. The czar delights in mass executions. All loyal to him must attend his little 'ceremonies.' "

"I—" Slocum began. He had taken a step backward. His heel caught on something softer than rock. Craning around and looking down, he stared at a man's arm. A dead man's arm.

He shone the light directly into the corpse's face. The man was undoubtedly Russian but unlike Mikhail, he was richly dressed in the fashion of a nobleman. But his death was as cruel as Mikhail's. He had been shot in the middle of the back.

12

"Yuri!" Anastasia exclaimed, seeing the body.

"You know him?" asked Slocum, his eyes flashing from the corpse to a spot deeper in the cave. He had been sure that this was the one with the pit holding Mikhail's body. Since he had been wrong about that, he was probably wrong about the feeling that deeper in the cave presented no danger. Whoever had killed Yuri had not exited the cave; Slocum could tell from the muddy marks on the cavern floor.

"It is Yuri Balushkin," she said with such venom that Slocum's attention snapped back to the duchess.

"What's he to you? Another servant?" From the way the dead man dressed, Slocum doubted Balushkin had ever worked for her. If anything, he had a legion of servants of his own to tend his every whim.

"He is nothing," Anastasia said. This time her lip curled and she started to spit on the body, then thought better of it. "Leave him. We have Mikhail to find. He was an honorable man, but not this one."

"Could Balushkin have been wandering around in the caves?" he asked, thinking of how he and Elizabeth had been stranded when someone set fire to the twine. He had seen shadows moving but had no idea as to who it might have been. From the way he was curled up into a ball, Balushkin's height wasn't easily discerned, but he might have topped six feet. That squared with the impression Slocum had of the man he had pursued.

"If so, he was looking for the devil himself to make a deal with," Anastasia said. She started to leave, but Slocum reached out and grabbed her arm, stopping her.

"Spill it," Slocum said. "Everything. Why are you here and who is Balushkin? We were ambushed at the deserted mine. Who wanted Mikhail dead?"

"Those are too many questions to answer here, John," she said, looking past him into the tunnel. "My words might be heard miles from here."

Slocum realized she was right. He remembered how his words had echoed until the incessant wind had blotted them out. If he had shouted down one of the tunnels lacking the stiff breeze, those words might still be rolling along for someone to hear.

Slocum started to search Balushkin, then realized the body wasn't going anywhere. Whoever had murdered the man would already have plundered the body and taken anything of value or interest.

He stepped out into the late-day light and looked around, trying to figure how he had gone wrong. The landmarks were all wrong when he looked at the countryside from this angle, but he thought he recognized a peak in the Black Hills off to the north that would give a guidepost to the actual resting place for Mikhail's body.

Anastasia shouted to her two Cossacks and the three servants. They immediately wheeled the wagon around and headed for a stand of piñon a quarter mile off.

"That is a good place to camp," Anastasia said. She watched as the wagon clattered and rolled off, saying nothing for several seconds. When she was certain the servants were out of earshot, she said, "Yuri Balushkin is a thief and a traitor to the czar!"

Slocum wondered why this information was something to be kept from her attendants, then realized there was something more to the man's death that bothered Anastasia.

"Were you lovers?" he asked.

Her dark eyes flashed as she stared pointedly at him. Her body was rigid and her teeth ground together unconsciously. This was as angry as Slocum had seen the Russian duchess, telling him his shot in the dark had hit a bull's-eye.

"He betrayed me. He used me and then stole the czar's golden scepter, the supreme symbol of Romanov rule."

"This scepter," Slocum asked. "It's worth a lot?"

"There is no amount of money that can replace it. The scepter is *the* symbol of Romanov power. A few pounds of gold, a handful of jewels, that is nothing that cannot be replaced. But Alexander must have the scepter before summer rituals require him to appear with it. If the peasants see their czar without it, they will claim he is not the true ruler of all the Russias and revolt."

"You mean whoever helped Balushkin will prod them into revolting," Slocum said. "Nobody overthrows a ruler because he doesn't have a gold scepter."

Anastasia laughed harshly. "You know nothing of Russia. We are a people of great ceremony. If anything disturbs our people, shaking their confidence in their czar, there will be hell to pay. Soldiers would even rebel against orders to keep order and join the serfs if they do not see the scepter in Alexander's firm grip."

Slocum began to understand. The peasants could be brutally kept down—but that required the might of the Russian army. It was the soldiers who would turn the tide of power in the country if Czar Alexander appeared for any ceremony without the scepter.

"Pounds?" Slocum asked, not caring about any Russian ruler's head. "Did you say the scepter is made from *pounds* of gold?"

"Da," she said, her accent thicker as emotion washed over her. "Ten pounds, at least."

"But you're more worried about the czar not carrying it next summer?"

"What's a few thousand dollars' worth of gold and jewels to the czar?" she said in an offhand manner.

"Why did Balushkin bring it here?"

Anastasia thought a moment before speaking. "He escaped with other outlaws across Siberia, knowing the czar would watch carefully any path into Europe. He crossed the Bering Straits and came down through Canada. I suspect he intended to meet a buyer of artifacts here."

"An American?"

Anastasia shrugged. It did not matter to her who the buyer might be. All that she focused on was retrieving the czar's symbol of authority and preventing an uprising.

"Why can't the czar have another scepter made? The peasants wouldn't know the difference." Slocum's answer was a harsh snort of disgust at his ignorance.

"They would know," Anastasia said. "There are nobles, like Balushkin, who would be certain the serfs knew."

"Where do you think this scepter is?" Slocum asked. "In these caves?"

"I knew we were close to Balushkin but did not know he was this close," she said, looking past Slocum to the mouth of the cave. Her lips curled back as if she wanted to spit again. "Perhaps he met with the buyer, who double-crossed him. Such is the term, is it not?"

"It happens," Slocum allowed. "It's odd that a man clever enough to steal a prized possession of the czar and then evade a hunt across Russia would fall such easy prey to an American desperado."

"I can understand it," Anastasia said. "We Russians

have some contempt for you rustic Americans. Yuri would think you little better than savages, beneath his contempt." Anastasia paused, then smiled almost shyly. "Until I met you, I thought the same things about Americans."

Slocum smiled without humor. He had done nothing to merit her admiration. He couldn't even backtrack on his own trail to find her dead servant.

"Balushkin must have hidden it. Perhaps he was murdered when he would not reveal the spot," Anastasia said. Her enthusiasm grew as the notion of finding the scepter became more of a reality. "We can go into the caves and find where he cached it."

Slocum fell silent. The idea of getting lost underground again didn't appeal to him, even if he might recover the scepter for Anastasia. A few thoughts of getting the golden scepter and keeping it for himself died in Slocum's mind. He wasn't that kind. He had no interest in keeping a czar who was likely a despot on the throne, but Anastasia was earnest in wanting to find and return the royal symbol. That meant Slocum wouldn't steal it from under her nose.

What he intended was to never go into those caves again. Riding back south looked to be more of a good way to spend his time. Staring at the sky, even one as obscured with snow clouds as this was, appealed more to him that choking on a smoky lantern that revealed nothing but tons of rock over his head.

"Oh, good, they have pitched my tent," Anastasia said.

Slocum looked ahead at the stand of trees. He almost laughed out loud. A huge parti-colored tent flapped in the cold wind blowing through the Black Hills.

"That's more elegant than the room you took in Goldust," Slocum said, not bothering to keep the irony from his words.

Anastasia smiled knowingly. She beckoned him on.

The two rode to the tent where two servants hurried over
to take the reins so they could go into the tent. The two
Cossacks stood guard just inside the flap. The third servant worked at a small fire in the center of the tent, heat-
ing water for tea.

"Excellent timing," Anastasia said. "Tea."

The silver samovar steamed as the servant poured the
tea into bone china cups with fancy gold rims.

"I'll leave you to your tea, Duchess," Slocum said,
aware that the Cossacks were eying him suspiciously. It
didn't matter to them that he had their duchess's approval.
They were entrusted with her safety and Slocum was an
unknown, an American barbarian.

"Nonsense. Sit there," Anastasia said, pointing to
fluffed pillows near the samovar. "Serve us, Dmitri."

The servant carefully poured tea that looked strong
enough to take the paint off a board. Slocum hesitated,
then realized hot tea or even hot water would go down
his gullet well. He had spent too much time out in the
bitter wind freezing his bones through and through.

"Thanks," Slocum said, dropping down so he could
keep the two Cossacks in view. He didn't want to shoot
it out with them but would if they made any move against
him. "I'll have some, then I've got to be on the trail."

"Without retrieving poor Mikhail's body?" Anastasia
asked lightly. She sipped at her tea and then languorously
lounged back on the cushions like some potentate. Slocum
realized this was the way Anastasia lived back in Russia.
Servants and fancy teacups, furnishings worth enough to
keep him alive for a year. He and Anastasia came from
different worlds.

"I'll find the body," Slocum promised. "Then I'll be
off."

"To where it is warmer? Southward, perhaps?" Anastasia's dark eyes studied him over the rim of her cup.
"You will not help find the czar's scepter?"

"Not my fight," Slocum said.

"You forget so easily? Who was it that killed your friend Scoggins?"

Slocum bit at his lower lip when she hit him with that small fact. He had forgotten about Matt Scoggins in the rush of everything that had happened. Simply staying alive had forced his friend's memory deeper into his brain. Until now.

"I owe Matt," he said. "But I don't know that finding the scepter will help bring his killer to justice. Maybe Yuri Balushkin was the one who killed him."

"Yuri was capable of such treachery," Anastasia said. "Yuri also had others with him equally capable of such murder."

Slocum felt as if he had gotten himself caught on fly-paper. The more he wanted to leave the Dakotas the more reasons surfaced keeping him here. Finding the scepter need not be part of it, especially if he had to go underground again. Slocum had his fill of being buried alive in those winding, rambling tunnels.

"Our goals might be different but the road we travel to our own ends is the same, John," she said, setting down the teacup and moving over by Slocum. He looked up and saw the two Cossacks and Dmitri had left. He hadn't even noticed them go.

"They know their place," Anastasia answered his unspoken question.

"Like I do?" asked Slocum, knowing he was being pulled into the beautiful duchess's spider web.

"I hope you know your proper place," she said in a husky voice. She moved a little closer and closed her eyes, waiting in anticipation for what she read on Slocum's face.

He kissed her hard on the lips. The exquisite Russian responded in kind, pressing her warm breasts against him. Slocum kissed her lips and eyes and nibbled on her earlobes until Anastasia purred like a contented cat. Then he worked down her throat and began kissing the flesh exposed as he unfastened her blouse one inch at a time.

When the final tie came free, Anastasia's breasts popped free like giant hills waiting to be conquered. Slocum set about doing just that. His lips kissed and his teeth lightly nipped, and when he reached the pink-capped summits, he suckled hard. Anastasia writhed under him, thrusting her chest up to get more of her breasts into his mouth as he moved from one to the other.

Slocum gripped them firmly and slowly moved up to the summit, forcing along the excited blood pounding in her veins. The pink nubs of her nipples hardened to the point Slocum could feel her hammering heart when he pressed his tongue down hard.

"More, John, give me more, so much more," she cooed. Her fingers laced through his lank hair, guiding him here and there so he would know what thrilled her the most.

But Slocum had ideas of his own. He stripped off her blouse and left her bare to the waist, then began working on her skirts. Fumbling a little prompted Anastasia to help.

"Let me," she said. "And you should get naked, too."

Slocum had other ideas on how to occupy his time. As she worked on the clever fastenings, he hiked up her skirts and started kissing along the insides of her legs, working his head higher and higher. By the time Anastasia had shucked off her skirts, Slocum had found paradise nestled between her legs. His tongue lashed out, dragged up and down her nether lips, then plunged into her.

This was one delicate cave he did not mind exploring.

As his tongue waggled around, she thrashed about like a fish out of water. Her words slurred and she moaned more loudly as passions mounted inside her trim, lush young body. When his tongue stabbed out and whirled about inside her moist tightness, Anastasia lifted her rump off the pillows and ground her crotch down into his face. Slocum gave as good as he received and was rewarded with the woman's low, guttural cries of released pleasure.

As she sank down, spent, Slocum began stripping off his own clothing. Anastasia watched every bit of his raiment being tossed aside and recovered some of her energy for what was to come.

"You are so strong," she said, running her hands over his powerfully muscled body. Here and there, she traced around scars, from knives, from bullets, from longhorns that had moved quicker than Slocum. But always her hands drifted downward until he revealed his erect manhood.

Anastasia's fingers closed about him, and she started to use her mouth on him as he had on her.

"No," he said, reaching out. His strong hands gripped the woman's hips. With a quick move, he flipped her over onto her belly so her lily-white, perfectly shaped bottom pointed upward. He stroked over the half-moons, then gripped them firmly and began kneading as if they were hunks of bread dough. Again he found the right way to excite the duchess.

"Yes, John, my body's on fire. Inside, I burn for you!"

"I haven't even started to stoke your fire yet," he told her. He lifted her off the pillows so she was on hands and knees. Slocum moved behind her, poked forward with his iron shaft and found the wet slit where his mouth had been a few minutes earlier. With a mighty shove forward, he sank deep into her yielding interior.

Again the duchess cried out. She tossed her long black mane like a frisky filly, then sobbed in pleasure when he reached around and under her to cup her breasts. He fondled those milky globes while remaining fully inside her clenched female passage. Temblors built in her body and threatened to become an earthquake.

Only then did Slocum begin withdrawing from his snug

berth. The friction of his reentry sent both their pulses racing. He continued to fondle and stroke and explore every bare inch of her white body, but the motion in and out was wearing on him. Anastasia used her strong inner muscles to clamp firmly, to tease and torment and urge him on.

Slocum began stroking faster. When Anastasia tossed her long black hair back, Slocum caught it up like the reins of a horse. He used the very tips of the hair to stroke along the woman's back, giving her gentle, bedeviling stimulation while his thick manhood rammed back and forth like the piston on a steam engine.

When Slocum's hands began to quake, he knew he was reaching the point of no return. He stroked faster. He felt the expected explosion deep within the duchess at the same time she let out a timber wolf's cry of pure pleasure. Crotch smashing into her rump, grinding around and then thrilling to the rush of heat within him, Slocum rode out the sexual delight until he couldn't go on any longer.

He flopped onto the pillows, sweaty and tired out from the lovemaking. Anastasia fell facedown onto the pillows and lay panting for breath for a minute or two, then rolled over and pressed her naked body tightly against his.

"You are a magnificent stallion like those that roam wild on the steppes," she said. "Never can you be broken. And never will I try." Anastasia let out a tiny sigh of resignation.

Slocum knew he would help her find the czar's scepter. How much harder could that be than finding Matt Scoggins's killer?

13

"Damn," Slocum muttered under his breath. The landmark crag he had spotted the day before proved to be a red herring. From the top of the rise, he looked out over forested land covered in knee-deep snow. Three or four small vents to the cavern system below spewed out cool air warmed in the bowels of the earth, but nowhere did he see the cave opening where he had left Mikhail's body.

"We can look more later after we eat," Anastasia said. The Russian duchess tried to keep her temper in check, but Slocum knew she was getting madder by the minute at his failure to find her servant's corpse. He didn't much blame her.

"Go ahead and pitch camp," he said. "I'll find a local to guide us. If I can't get someone who knows the lay of the land, I'll buy a map. There must be a dozen of them in a boomtown."

"Such maps are worthless, John," Anastasia said. "I know. I have bought many of them since coming here. No two agree. Thieves scribble out directions for the unwary and sell these maps at high prices. They stopped selling to me because of Mikhail."

Slocum nodded, understanding what she meant. The

first few no-accounts selling bogus maps to her might get away with it. The wrath of the giant Mikhail would quickly stop others from trying to take advantage of her. He exhaled hotly, watching his breath turned to silvery plumes in the cold air before vanishing entirely. There might be maps, but a guide was better.

"It'll speed up our hunt," Slocum declared.

"I asked and found no one willing to guide an expedition into the Black Hills," she said. "I offered a great amount of money, also."

"Scoggins took you up on the offer," Slocum pointed out.

When she didn't answer, he finished the thought for her. Matt Scoggins had been willing to guide her, and someone who wanted to keep her in Goldust away from the scepter had murdered him. Slocum wasn't sure how well Scoggins knew this land, but it might have been pretty well if he had poked around looking for a gold strike.

"I can find my way back here," Slocum said. "I won't be longer than a day or two."

"If you do not come back?" Anastasia asked, her dark eyes icier than the landscape. She thought he was going to desert her.

"I'll be back. If I'm not, track down my body and bury me up by Scoggins." With that, Slocum wheeled his horse and lit out for the road leading back to Goldust. He wasn't sure if Anastasia would do as he asked, but it hardly mattered what she did now. He had taken on the hunt for the scepter as a matter of personal honor. Slocum figured if he found the czar's scepter he would also find the backshooter who had murdered Scoggins.

Everything tied together, all the threads leading to the gold scepter.

Slocum got on the road in less than an hour and rode steadily, arriving in Goldust by midafternoon. He went immediately to the land office and poked his head inside. An assayer worked diligently, pouring blue liquid over rocks until they sizzled and popped. The man hunted for something that wasn't there because he grunted in disgust, tossed the mess into a trash can and started his assay on a new sample.

"You got a map of the area?" Slocum asked. The chemist jumped as if Slocum had poked him in the ribs. He had been so intent on his work that he hadn't heard anyone come in.

"Map? You're crazy. Nobody's got one of the area. The cavalry might, but the nearest fort is a hundred miles off. Not likely they give a good goddamn."

"How do you record land claims?"

"In this book," the chemist said. "I double as county clerk, as far as there even is a county. Somebody comes in with a claim, I take the money and write down the details here."

Slocum swung the book around and studied it for a moment. He had seen his share of recorded land deeds in his day, but this one was the most outrageous. The assayer did exactly as he claimed. He made no effort to record the actual position but took as gospel what the miners said.

"How do you keep claims from overlapping?" Slocum asked.

The man shrugged and said, "Ain't my call. If the prospectors want to fight it out, they can."

Slocum saw that the assay agent served no good purpose in Goldust other than to make the prospectors think they had a legitimate claim. A dozen miners could lay claim to the same stretch of rock and never know it until they banged heads digging out the rock.

"I need a guide. Someone who knows the country south of town."

"South? You mean west. That's where the big strikes

are now. The ones east of here petered out real quick."
He pulled a thick book from under the desk where he
worked and dropped it with a bang onto the counter.
"Them's the claims out east. Ain't a one still bringing in
ore to test."

"There must be an old-timer here. A mountain man or
scout for the cavalry?"

"Nope, most of them folks got fed up when Goldust
started growing like Topsy. Moved on to less populated
parts."

Slocum left, knowing the assayer was probably right
about finding anyone in Goldust who had done any ex-
tensive scouting. Still, he had to try. His belly protested
not getting any food since breakfast, although that had
been a mighty fine meal with Anastasia from her stores.
Slocum saw that his horse would be taken care of for an
exorbitant price, then went into a saloon to order a beer
or two and have a sandwich.

As he drank and ate, he asked any who came in if they
knew of guides willing to work for top wages. He saw
the flash of greed in many eyes, then fade when they
realized they had to deal with a man who wore a Colt
Navy slung gunfighter fashion and who might be a tad
angry if they tried to cheat him.

By the time Slocum had eaten his fill, he realized he
wasn't going to find a guide in Goldust. The lure of striking it rich with a huge gold discovery blotted out momentary gain. About everyone he talked to had recently
arrived. No one who had prowled the hills and might
know the caves underground was left in Goldust.

Slocum stepped into the gathering gloom, looked at the
sky and heaved a sigh. For the first time he could remember, the sky was clear, save for a few wispy clouds drifting across the stars trying to poke through the velvet
night. No storm. No snow.

He retrieved his horse and mounted. The mare was in

better fettle after a currying and some grain. He rode from town, going north. The gold fields were west and the eastern area had been exhausted. This was the only direction where he might find people knowledgeable about the region.

Whether any of them would be willing to act as guide was something Slocum had to determine for himself.

Around midnight he caught the scent of burning pine. He rode slowly now, aware that he might spook the Sioux camped here. The Indians had no need for gold and did not understand the white man's greed when it came to the yellow metal. But they did range throughout the area seeking buffalo and fighting their skirmishes with other tribes. If anyone knew their way around the caves, it would be the Sioux.

Slocum stopped a hundred yards from the camp where a half dozen small fires burned fitfully. He saw their tepees as shadows, barely outlined against even darker trees. Starlight was intermittent tonight because of the thin, drifting clouds, so Slocum sat astride his horse in the middle of a meadow and waited. As he bided his time, he took out the fixings and rolled himself a cigarette, using material he had bought in Goldust.

He finished smoking the first one and started on a second when a lone figure stalked out to speak to him.

"Howdy," Slocum greeted.

"What you want?" the Sioux brave said in passable English. He sounded surly and had both hands on knife handles, the blades thrust through a broad leather belt beaded in the style of a chief. Slocum doubted the brave was a chief himself but might have taken this as booty in some long-ago battle.

"Would you like a smoke?" Slocum held up his bag of tobacco, letting it spin slowly so the man saw it.

"You would smoke with me?"

"Of course," Slocum said.

The brave motioned impatiently for Slocum to dismount. They settled down on their haunches. The brave took Slocum's tobacco and rolling papers, expertly building a smoke of his own. He let Slocum light the cigarette and silently worked on it, clouds of smoke rising around him as if he were a steam engine rather than a simple warrior.

"We hunt," the brave finally said. "Why you here?"

Slocum carefully explained how he needed a guide before entering the caves south of Goldust. He let the Sioux make another cigarette and get it lit from the dying coals of his first smoke.

"Do you know of those caves where the ground breathes?" Slocum asked.

The Sioux nodded once.

"Could you guide me through the caves? Much tobacco. Much white man food." Slocum had decided the band of Sioux were hunters rather than a war party, in spite of the brave's fierce demeanor and constant threatening with his knives.

"No caves," the Sioux said firmly. "No go into caves."

"Why? Are they sacred?"

"Not sacred. Nothing there. No reason to go. No game. No hiding."

"You're not afraid? Because of the constant wind that comes from the cave openings?"

The Sioux leaped to his feet. "I am Hopping Bird. I take ten scalps in war! Not afraid!"

"But you won't show me how to get through the caves? Where the entrances are and how to get out again?"

"Know nothing of caves. Not go there. Ever."

Slocum let this denial hang in the cold night air for a spell, then nodded and stood. He held out the remainder of his tobacco.

"Thanks."

Hopping Bird hesitated a moment, then grabbed the

small canvas bag as if Slocum might try to pull it away.

"You go now?"

"If Hopping Bird doesn't know his way through the caves, no one else among the Sioux does," Slocum said. He waited for a denial.

The Indian nodded once, signaling the powwow was at an end. Disheartened that his last attempt to find a local guide had failed, Slocum climbed back onto his horse and headed slowly back for Goldust. He thought hard as he rode. There had been no sign of Indians inside the caves, leading him to believe Hopping Bird had told the truth. For whatever reason, religious or otherwise, the Sioux simply did not enter the caves. They might know where the ground snorted out its constant breath but once inside the caves, they would be as ill-equipped to find any-thing—or anyone—as Slocum.

Bone tired and resigned to going it on his own to find where Mikhail's body had been left, Slocum returned to Goldust just after sunrise. He needed sleep but wanted to get back to Anastasia as quickly as possible. He was honor bound to help her get back her ruler's symbol of power as much as he was to find Matt Scoggins's killer.

But a hot meal and a few minutes of shut-eye wouldn't slow his return that much. As he dismounted in front of the small café where he had eaten before, he saw the assayer arguing with a man in front of the claims office down the street.

When the assayer pointed at Slocum and the man turned to look, time stood still for a moment.

Recognition flooded Slocum. He knew this gent. His hand went for his gun, although the distance was too great for a good shot. He had winged him twice after running off the man who had rifled his saddlebags in the cave when he had first arrived in Dakota Territory.

The assay agent grabbed the man's shoulders and spun him around, then shoved him down an alley.

"Wait!" Slocum cried, tearing down the street as he dragged out his hogleg. He brought up his six-shooter but didn't fire. The outlaw had vanished from sight, leaving only the assay agent standing on the boardwalk outside his office.

"Who was that?" Slocum demanded, skidding to a halt in front of the assayer.

"I, uh, I don't know. Just a fellow who wanted to know about gold."

Slocum cocked his pistol and shoved it under the chemist's chin. The look of determination on his face spoke louder than any words. If answers weren't quick in coming, the chemist would lose his life.

"He's, uh, he calls himself Cactus John Coltrane. That's all I know! Honest!"

"You never had an honest thought or did an honest deed in your miserable life," Slocum said, shoving the man back against the rough-hewn plank wall of his assay office. "Who's his partner?"

"Petersen?" The assayist clamped his mouth shut tightly when he realized Slocum had duped him into revealing even more.

"Coltrane and Petersen. What's their game?"

"I don't know. Honest." Seeing Slocum's reaction at using this word again, the assayist swallowed hard and held out his hands, palms toward Slocum. "Look, I don't know what they're up to. They bring in ore now and again for me to test. That's all I know."

"Claim jumpers?" Things fit together for Slocum now. Coltrane and Petersen robbed miners, probably leaving them for dead, and stole their gold. The assayist bought the stolen gold from them, using it for his own purposes. Slocum wondered how many vaunted high-test claims held nothing but drossy rock. The chemist could salt the claims and see that they sold for fantastic amounts on the basis of the gold he got from Coltrane and Petersen. He

probably split the sale price down the middle with those
who wanted to sell worthless claims.

Or he might have some even more complicated confidence game running. Boomtowns were rife with fraudu-
lent schemes, and the assayist was in the perfect position
to profit. He turned out ore assays any way he wanted and
even acted as the county land agent, recording claims and
possibly determining where the juiciest profits were to be
made.

For a price. Always for a hefty price.

Slocum doubted the man was going to hightail it from
Goldust when he had so many suckers to cheat. Men like
the assayist always figured they could buy off trouble and
wouldn't think Slocum was any different. If it turned out
he had anything to do with either Coltrane or Petersen
killing Matt Scoggins, he would find out differently.

Slocum looked down the muddy alley where Coltrane
had fled, then took out after him. He rounded the back of
the assay office in time to see the man mounting a sway-
backed horse.

"Stop or I'll shoot!" Slocum called and shot anyway.
The bullet missed its target and lent added speed to the
horse's flying hooves.

Slocum fired twice more, then saw the fleeing outlaw
was too far off for even a lucky shot to hit. He reversed
his course and ran back to where he had left his horse.
Vaulting into the saddle, he rode hard after the owlhoot
he had shot twice before.

He couldn't even remember when it had been since so
much had happened after he had found the windy cave in
the snowstorm. But Slocum never forgot a face of any
man who took a shot at him. He rode harder and found
tracks through the snow to the east of town that were so
easy to follow he almost laughed.

The frightened outlaw made no attempt to stick to the
muddy, cut-up track that was the road leading into Gol-

dust. If he stayed off the road and in the pristine snow-banks, Slocum had all winter long—or at least until the next snowfall—to find him.

Slocum reined in and gave his horse a rest, alternately walking and trotting it when he got to level patches of land. The tracks led straight across a meadow to a stand of trees. With the sun coming up over the trees, Slocum headed for the junipers. As he pulled the brim of his hat down to shade his eyes, a cold realization blasted through him.

He made the same mistake a greenhorn would.

The sound of the rifle shot and the feel of the bullet ripping into his body came at the same time. Slocum tumbled sideways off his horse and crashed facedown to the snowy ground.

14

Wind roared in Slocum's ears when there wasn't any blowing. Nothing but white showed in front of his face, and every muscle in his body ached terribly. The skin on his face began to tingle from frostbite, making him realize that he was still alive, no matter how bad he felt. He clutched his fingers and came up with two small snowballs, then he relaxed and forced himself to lie still. Memories flooded him now, and he knew how precarious his position was out in the middle of the meadow. His horse nervously pawed the snowy ground a few yards away, smelling blood but not sure if she should panic and run. There was no way he could reach the horse and escape back the way he had come before the sniper took him out of the saddle again.

Slocum turned his head slightly so he could see back toward the trees. A pair of men walked out, both carrying rifles. Slocum tried to guess which one was marksman enough to hit him at such a distance. Coltrane? Petersen? It didn't matter. Both were dead men.

His body heat began melting the snow around him. The approaching men might turn anxious seeing that he wasn't turning the same temperature as the snow in which he lay.

Worse, Slocum worried that his six-shooter might be clogged with mud. The delicate mechanism of the Colt Navy required constant maintenance. He had been careful to remove all oil and grease from the metal to keep it from freezing in the cold winter but that was some time ago.

He inched his hand down his side and under his body until he clutched the pistol firmly. He felt warmth dripping across his arm. He knew the bullet had hit him but had been deflected by the heavy duster he wore. Still, the tumbling slug had grazed his side and left a bloody gash along his ribs that made breathing painful.

Slocum sucked in a deep lungful of air, let the pain jolt him into full consciousness, then rolled onto his back and fired in the same motion. His first bullet went high and took off the hat of the man he recognized now as Coltrane. Coltrane reacted foolishly by turning to grab his flying hat.

Slocum's next bullet ended the man's foul life.

His partner stared at his fallen friend, then looked over at Slocum before turning tail and running for the shelter of the junipers. Slocum wondered if the man had a death wish. He sat up painfully, winced at the jolt of fierce agony in his side, then steadied his six-gun with both hands and squeezed the trigger.

The Colt misfired. Slocum cocked and fired again. This time the hammer fell on an empty chamber.

Cursing, he forced his way to his feet. The running man had reached the edge of the forest and disappeared into its sheltering protection.

Slocum whistled for his horse. The mare came over hesitantly, then let Slocum mount. He twisted about to reach into his saddlebags and almost passed out from the pain in his side. He caught himself, found the oilskin pouch with spare loaded cylinders for his six-shooter and drew out the two spares. He kicked out the emptied one from his gun, wrapped it carefully in the oilcloth, loaded his Colt and tucked the spare cylinder into an inner pocket.

He was loaded for bear and ready to track down the owlhoot who had tried to rob and kill him. Slocum rode past Coltrane's body and never looked back, intent on the dark woods ahead. He damned himself for falling for such a simple ambush. The sun in his eyes, the dark woods, the easy shot across level ground—it had been perfect for them. If he'd had his wits about him, he would have skirted the meadow and come up on them along the fringes of the forest so he would never have presented such an easy target.

Slocum had no trouble finding where Petersen had gone into the woods. From the length of his stride, Petersen was running hell-bent-for-leather. He knew, after seeing his partner cut down, what his fate would be if he didn't put miles and miles between himself and Slocum.

Turning cautious now, Slocum dismounted and followed on foot to the spot where the men had tethered their horses. Petersen had left Coltrane's gelding behind in his haste to get away. Slocum had to laugh when he saw evidence that Petersen had been in such a rush that he had ridden into a low hanging branch and had knocked himself out of the saddle.

The tree limbs were so low in the young-growth forest that Slocum preferred to stay on foot and lead his horse rather than duck constantly. Bending over proved increasingly painful for him because of his wound, and after ten minutes hiking Slocum grew light-headed and knew he had to tend his wound before going on. Petersen was leaving a trail a blind man could follow. Slocum thought even on his best day Petersen wasn't half the frontiersman and tracker that Slocum was.

Peeling back his duster caused Slocum to gasp. The blood had dried and glued his duster to his shirt and the

shallow wound beneath. Using his knife, Slocum cut away
the cloth, cleaned the long, bloody gash the best he could
and then packed snow around it. The shock of cold against
his hot flesh made him woozy. When the dizziness passed,
Slocum felt like he could whip his weight in wildcats. Or
at least wildcat cubs.

He used strips torn from his shirt as a bandage, then
went after Petersen. As he had hoped, Petersen was so
frightened that he made no effort to hide his trail. Now
and then Slocum stopped and listened hard, hoping to hear
the running man. Only the soft sigh of wind through the
evergreens reached his ears. More on his mind than over-
taking him was not walking into another ambush. Men
like Petersen got one idea into their skulls and if it worked
once, they reckoned it would always work. It was up to
Slocum to be sure he didn't make the same mistake twice.

Emerging from the forest, Slocum saw that Petersen
had kept going in a straight path up the side of a steep,
rocky hill. The way it rose at its summit in a sharp needle-
like spire told Slocum the man had to go around rather
than over. He chose to skirt the base of the hill. In less
than an hour he saw Petersen struggling down the hillside
not fifty feet ahead of him. The man was so intent on
putting distance between his partner's killer and himself
that he never saw Slocum.

Slocum's first shot spooked Petersen's horse, causing
the animal to rear and paw in fright at thin air. The second
shot caused the horse to throw its rider and gallop away.
Slocum took his time riding over to the fallen man.

Petersen lay flat on his back, struggling to get air back
into his lungs. He reached for his six-shooter when he
saw Slocum towering above him, then froze. He stared
down the barrel of Slocum's freshly loaded six-shooter.

"You tried to dry-gulch me. Twice," Slocum said. "I
want information or I'll shoot you in both legs and leave
you out here to freeze." He glanced up at the sky and

shook his head. "A pity that won't be too long since there's another storm on the way. You'd freeze to death before you suffered much."

"Wait, no, you got this all wrong!"

"Oh?" Slocum said with mock civility. "How do I have it wrong that your partner, Cactus John Coltrane, tried to put a bullet through me back in the meadow? And that I'd winged him twice when you tried to backshoot me in a cave ten days ago?" Slocum wondered if the blood showed through his duster. It probably did. He shifted his weight a little so Petersen could get a good look at the blood stains and ragged tear where the bullet had ripped the tough canvas duster.

"Y-you know him?" The murderous outlaw reacted with enough shock for Slocum to know that he had hit the man hard.

"Your name's Petersen, isn't it? I know everything, including how you shot my partner in the back."

"We never did nothin' like that! How could we know Yuri was your partner?"

Slocum had expected Petersen to confess to gunning down Matt Scoggins. Yuri Balushkin's murder was the furthest thing from his mind. It was his turn to try to hide his surprise.

"You shot Balushkin?"

"No, no, that's what I'm tryin' to tell you. We never shot him. He was comin' out of that cave when somebody inside gunned him down. We never had a chance to kill him."

"Show me the cave," Slocum said, coming to a quick decision. He figured Petersen had a better knowledge of the caves and where Balushkin might be than he ever could. After they found the Russian's body, they could keep looking for Mikhail's.

"What do you care? He ain't got it on him. We looked."

"The scepter?" Again Slocum saw how he rocked the

outlaw. "I told you. I know everything, and if you try lying to me I'll cut your ears off, then stuff them down your throat till you choke."

"Mister, me and Cactus, we just blowed into Goldust. We never wanted to get mixed up in any of this, but a hunk of gold that big was too good to pass up. Can you blame us?"

Slocum needed Petersen to sort out the tangled web of who was gunning down the Russians—and who had killed Scoggins. He wasn't sure Petersen was telling the truth about any of it, not with the man's willingness to shoot anyone who moved. Right now, Slocum wanted to let things come out slowly.

"Get your horse," he said, motioning with his six-shooter. Slocum considered making Petersen bury his partner, then decided against it. Such a low-down snake didn't deserve a proper burial. The only prayer Slocum was likely to give over the dead man was one for the wolves not to get too sick when they picked his carcass clean.

"The countryside's all snowed in. Everything looks the same," Petersen started. He fell silent when he saw the expression on Slocum's face. Slocum was past letting the man jaw on endlessly about how little he knew. The only thing of importance was what Petersen *did* know.

After an hour of riding, Slocum began to identify landmarks around them and knew Petersen was taking them straight to the cave where Yuri Balushkin had been cut down. He hazarded a question to start the flow of information.

"How much exploring did you and Coltrane do inside the caves?"

"Not too much," Petersen said. "We didn't want to get lost. It's a regular maze down there." He chuckled. "While we were pokin' 'round, though, we did come across a lot of other folks. We figured they were all huntin' for the gold scepter, so we did what we could to get rid of them."

"Like setting fire to a few yards of twine?" Slocum asked.

Petersen chuckled "That was inspired. I saw the string layin' on the floor and thought whoever was at the other end'd never find their way out if I set fire to it. They must still be down in the caves lookin' for blue sky."

Petersen was too stupid to realize the only way Slocum could know was to have been at the other end of the twine.

"Who do you think shot Yuri?" asked Slocum.

"It wasn't me or Cactus John! We were tryin' to throw in with him to find the gold."

"He'd lost the scepter?"

"That's why he was hauntin' those caves day and night, not that you can tell which is which underground. We wanted to throw in with him, then double-cross him when we found the gold. He wouldn't even talk to us, then somebody shot him in the back."

"Who?"

Petersen frowned, then said, "Might have been Bartlett."

Again Slocum thought he was past surprise at the murderous ins and outs of this whole debacle.

"Ned or his wife?"

Petersen swung in the saddle and stared at him before saying, "That bitch is here? My God, if I'd knowed that, I'd never have stayed. There's no amount of gold worth tangling with her."

Slocum felt like a stranger moseying into a small town where everyone knew everyone else's business—and where they were all related by blood or marriage.

"How do you know her and Bartlett?"

"Everybody knows them, mister," Petersen said. "I wish I didn't, that's for certain."

Slocum looked around, got his bearings and made sure

they were riding directly for the cave where Anastasia had
insisted that they leave Yuri's body. The bright sunlight
shone off the moraines covered in snow, giving more
character to the land than he remembered. Not only were
there several cave openings nearby spewing out their
ceaseless supply of earth-warmed air, Slocum now saw
canyons branching off this broad U-shaped valley, going
into the towering hills in the distance.

"You know where Mikhail's body is?"

"He that dark-haired Russian woman's bodyguard?"
Petersen turned cautious, putting Slocum on guard that the
man was whipping up a new batch of lies.

Before Slocum could say a word, deafening gunfire
sounded. He had heard Gatling guns rattle their deadly
lead before, and this was close. He realized later that the
multitude of sound came from the initial muzzle blast that
was magnified by echoes from a narrow canyon mouth
some hundred yards away.

The torrent of lead kept Slocum busier than a beaver,
diving for cover. When the last of the echoes died down,
he was on the ground, near a cave mouth, and Petersen
lay flat on his back with more holes in him than Slocum
wanted to count. The man had taken the worst of the
ambush and had saved Slocum, more by pure bad luck
than any heroic intent on his part.

Slocum hunted for the spot where the sniper had fired
from and decided none of the caves were likely spots. But
the mouth of a canyon was perfect, though the distance
was great enough to force the killer to fire as fast as he
could hoping one of his bullets found a target.

Slocum wondered if the ambusher had killed the man
he had intended. Whether Slocum had also been a target
didn't matter. He set out after the shooter, leaving Petersen behind near the cave where Yuri Balushkin also lay.

15

Slocum approached the canyon mouth cautiously, knowing the steeper sides afforded a sniper a dozen good spots from which to take another shot. He was sure the man who had killed Petersen had been on the ground, but that didn't mean he didn't have a partner or two up in the rocks waiting for a clean shot. The walls rose and moved to either side as Slocum pushed deeper into the canyon, which proved to be little more than a throat to another valley.

The tracks of a single rider led Slocum through the pass into the new valley. His eyes widened when he saw the number of small vents—and what had to be the cave where Mikhail had been killed. The entire region was connected underground by caves and above by the narrow, short canyons.

But Slocum's sharp eyes followed the tracks until they came to an abrupt end in front of the cave he had sought with Anastasia. He shielded his eyes against the glare from the fields of pure white snow and focused on the rider.

"Bartlett," Slocum muttered. He wasn't surprised, unless it was that the man rode alone and not with his wife, also. Of the pair, Slocum knew the real power rode with Elizabeth Bartlett.

He snapped his reins and got the tired mare moving along the same path already taken by Bartlett. Slocum drew his Winchester from its sheath and tried to lever a round into the chamber. In his rush to get out the long gun, he had forgotten that the cold had frozen some small spot of grease or oil. The wrenching sound of metal on metal alerted Bartlett that he had someone on his tail.

The man let out a yelp audible a hundred yards away when he looked back and saw he was being pursued. Bartlett put the spurs to his horse. Slocum saw his chance for a shot at Bartlett evaporate and shoved his useless rifle back into the saddle scabbard. At this distance a shot with his trusty six-gun was out of the question, unless he wanted to give Ned Bartlett even more reason to run faster.

Slocum knew calling to Bartlett to halt would be a waste of breath. He put his head down and got as much speed from his mare as he could, but Bartlett had already dismounted and ducked into a cave opening by the time Slocum came within pistol range.

"Come on out, Bartlett," Slocum shouted, hoping to flush the man. Then he felt the faint puff of wind from the cave. Slocum stood in the stirrups and studied the area. Not a quarter mile off was the cave mouth Slocum believed to be the one where Anastasia's servant lay dead. He got his bearings, then dismounted and drew his six-shooter.

Slocum pressed one hand against the cold rock at the cave mouth and felt faint vibration. A man running might produce such a faint earthquake. Reasonably sure that Bartlett wasn't lying in wait to ambush him, Slocum spun into the cave with his six-gun leveled. All he saw was darkness. The cave made a sharp turn to the right, cutting off light from outside quickly.

Advancing cautiously, Slocum was swallowed by the inky black. His eyes adjusted to the darkness, and he listened hard but saw nothing and heard even less. Any echoing of footfalls on the rocky floor had faded with distance.

He groped about for a ledge holding miners' candles and found nothing. Slocum returned his six-shooter to its holster and backed from the cave into the eye-watering brilliance of the snowfields. He would be a sitting duck if he ventured after Bartlett. The man had spent weeks exploring the caves and obviously knew the maze well enough to make his way through this section without a candle. Too many traps, both natural and manmade, awaited Slocum if he pursued.

Slocum wondered how long it would take to get to the next cave mouth on the surface, and if he might intercept Bartlett there. Then he gave up on that notion. He had no idea how the caves were connected or if Bartlett even ran toward the most obvious surface feature. Slocum turned to Bartlett's horse and searched the saddlebags for any clue why he had gunned down Petersen—or if he had even intended the outlaw as his victim and had only missed Slocum. Nothing. Slocum took the man's rifle but wasn't going to steal his horse.

Some crimes deserved hanging and taking a man's horse, even a backshooting coward like Ned Bartlett, wasn't done. But Slocum saw no reason to leave the man the weapon to shoot someone else.

Slocum retraced his path through the rocky pass, went back to the cave where Yuri Balushkin had died, then tracked down Anastasia and her entourage. He was a little surprised to find the Russian duchess still camped where he had left her, thinking she would grow impatient and go off on her own.

"John," Anastasia said, eyes narrowed as she stared at him closely. "You have been wounded!"

Slocum felt a twinge in his left side where the bullet had creased him. He had forgotten about it until the raven-haired woman mentioned it.

"Shows what I had to go through getting back," he said with a laugh.

"You make light of this." She snapped her fingers and two servants rushed out of the tent. "Fetch hot water and clean bandages. Now!" she snapped at her servants. Imperiously, Anastasia pointed inside. Slocum knew there was no denying her.

"Get out of the shirt," she said. For a woman used to courtly affairs Anastasia showed no distaste for either the bloody graze wound or the filthy clothing he discarded. By the time Slocum had tossed aside his shirt, the hot water had arrived and Anastasia set about cleaning and bandaging the wound. Again she surprised him with her expert attention.

"You've done this before," Slocum guessed.

"Too many times," she said, critically studying her handiwork. "The wound had already begun to heal, just a little. But it would have become infected because it was not entirely cleaned."

"I was mighty busy," Slocum said. He went on to tell her of the shoot-out with Coltrane and Petersen and how Ned Bartlett had entered the picture yet again.

"This Bartlett does not know where the scepter is," Anastasia said, thinking hard on the matter. "Why would he lurk about the caves if he had so much gold?"

"He and his wife might not be the only ones in those caves," Slocum said. He remembered the tall, almost skeletal man who had searched his saddlebags when he had first stumbled into the cave during the blizzard. He had no idea where he fit in. Slocum knew he might have been a bit delirious then and had mistaken the man's thin body for one of the others in the deadly search for the czar's scepter, but he didn't think so.

"Yuri would not have many men with him. Traitors are not suffered lightly in the court," Anastasia said. "If any of his retainers accompanied him, they might have left once he died."

"They might not know their boss was shot down," Slocum said. "There's too much we need to know, but first I want to find Bartlett. He might not have the scepter, but he has plenty of information I want."

"Agreed," Anastasia said. "What is your plan?"

"The servants will remain in camp," Anastasia said, as if this were important to Slocum. He studied the three openings into the ground. The one in front of him had to be the cave where Mikhail had met his death. The other two were likely connected to this one. Otherwise, he saw no trace of entry points into the caverns below ground. Each of the two Cossacks with Anastasia would enter a different cave and begin their hunt for Bartlett and his wife. Slocum would go into this cave, once Mikhail was removed.

"I want to be sure Mikhail is still here," Slocum said, hitching up his holster and making certain his six-gun was riding easy.

Anastasia motioned. The two Cossacks brought ropes and followed Slocum into the cave. He stopped to light a lantern and then advanced warily. The floor of the cave had been scuffed up by dozens of feet passing by recently. Slocum couldn't distinguish once track from the other, but this place seemed right to him.

"There," he said, coming to an abrupt halt and holding up the lantern. The light angled down to the bottom of the pit where Mikhail still lay crumpled.

Anastasia spoke rapidly in Russian to the two Cossacks. They expertly tied ropes around rocks and worked their way down to the dead body. A few minutes later they dragged Mikhail out into the afternoon sunlight.

"Poor Mikhail," Anastasia said softly. "So loyal."

"Loyal to the death," Slocum said.

"We will bury him outside town, in the cemetery where it is consecrated," Anastasia said.

While the servants bustled about wrapping the corpse in canvas and preparing it for transport back to Goldust, Slocum cleaned his rifle of all grease and made certain the magazine fed cartridges smoothly into the chamber. A dozen times he levered rounds into his trusty Winchester until he was confident it wouldn't fail him again.

"A rifle in caves?" asked Anastasia, smiling slightly. "Would not a pistol be better?"

"The magazine holds more rounds," Slocum said. "I don't expect to have to do more than shoot straight ahead, either."

"That might be a good choice," Anastasia said skeptically, "but what of the loud report?" She shivered delicately at the thought of bringing down tons of rock.

"The caves look secure enough," Slocum said. "A rifle report isn't going to do any more damage than a six-shooter."

"You expect a long fight?"

"I'm planning for one but not expecting it," he said. With the sturdy Cossacks, two pistols shoved into their broad leather belts, ready to enter the caves with him, any fight with Bartlett or his wife was likely to be over fast.

"You continue to amaze me, John," she said. "When first I saw you, I thought you were like any other cowboy. Impetuous, bullheaded, even stupid. But you are cautious when it is to your benefit, brave and never stupid."

Slocum snorted at that, sending a thick cloud of condensation gusting outward from his face. It was stupid going into these caves after a man and woman who had shown how capable they were of killing. So far, all he had to show for his effort was a wound in his side and a bloody trail of dead bodies. Of the lot, he'd miss Scoggins the most, but he also regretted Mikhail's death. The stocky Russian giant had been a man anyone would count himself lucky as having known.

"You two ready?" Slocum called to the Cossacks. They never moved a muscle, standing with their arms crossed until Anastasia rattled off a series of sharp commands in Russian. The two took off like she had lit a fire under them.

"They do not understand English well," Anastasia said.

"What you mean is, they won't obey anyone but you. That might get to be a problem," Slocum said.

"They know what to do," she said.

Slocum watched as the two split and went to the smaller entrances leading into the system of caves. He turned and fumbled with his lantern, heard a sound and looked up.

"Damnation!" He dropped the lantern and went for his rifle laying on the ground, getting it out but not firing.

"What is it, John?" Anastasia asked anxiously.

"I saw someone in the cave. It looked like the same owlhoot who'd tried to rob me when I took shelter from the blizzard just after I'd ridden into the Black Hills."

Anastasia lit the lantern as Slocum advanced, Winchester ready for action. The blackness of the cave swallowed up the painfully thin apparition he had spotted. As the duchess came up behind him, light from the lantern shone forth and bathed the rock in a fairy light. The man had vanished as if he had never existed.

"Perhaps you see a mirage?" she asked.

Slocum didn't bother answering. He knew what he had seen. There was yet another player in the deadly game within the caves.

"Give me the lantern," he said, reaching back with his left hand to take the handle. Anastasia passed it over, and Slocum started forward. He knew this stretch of rock intimately now and stopped at the edge of the pit where Mikhail had lain dead for so long. He judged the distance across the pit and then studied the sides of the tunnel. A small ledge afforded a way across without making a difficult leap.

He sidled along, duster scraping the rock until he got to the other side. A rock tumbling into the pit behind him caused Slocum to whirl around, rifle leveled.

"Anastasia! What are you doing? Get back to the wagon."

"Mikhail was my retainer," she said. "I will see that justice is done."

"This isn't going to be a picnic," Slocum said. "I've already lost sight of a man who stood less than ten feet away from me. If I miss a side corridor anywhere in this maze, I'm likely to get shot in the back like Yuri or stabbed in the belly like Mikhail."

"Then it is to your benefit to have someone watch that fine, strong back of yours," Anastasia said, smiling just a little. "You will have to do your best to be certain you do not get gutted by that bitch who killed Mikhail." The dark-haired beauty pushed her furred cap back on her forehead a little and wiped at sweat. "I am unused to the higher temperature in this cave, even if it is only that of a spring day."

"Get back. I can't watch you and hunt for Bartlett, too."

Anastasia laughed at him. "You have forgotten an important detail of cave explorations," she said. "My Cossacks know of such techniques. You need me to help out."

"What do you mean?" Slocum was getting edgy, dividing his attention between Anastasia and the sounds of the incessant wind blowing from deep within the earth. He could believe that wind was born in hell and was being spit out the devil's mouth.

She held up a piece of chalk.

"What's that for?"

"This," she said, making an arrow showing the direction into the cave. "You need only follow the marks back to return to this spot."

"Bartlett might erase them," Slocum said.

"It will be a tedious chore. From what you say of this Bartlett and his harridan wife, are they so meticulous?"

"Reckon not," Slocum said. He felt the pressure of time weighing down on him now. The living skeleton of a man was long gone, but he hadn't been the object of the search. Ned and Elizabeth Bartlett were the ones he wanted.

"I will mark our course, you will watch for danger. If you like, I will also carry the lantern, though that would make seeing new pits in the floor difficult for you."

"Take my rifle," Slocum said, starting to pass it over. Again Anastasia laughed at him.

"I am Russian. I will depend on weapons I know best." She pulled back her heavy coat to show she carried a brace of pistols like those carried by her Cossacks. Slocum didn't bother asking if she knew how to use them.

He was certain she did.

Without any further palaver, Slocum gripped his rifle in his right hand, held the lantern high with his left and set off into the depths of the caves to find the czar's gold scepter, the Bartletts—and answers.

16

Slocum's nerves turned rawer with every step he took. Anastasia trailed a few yards behind, the rasp of chalk against the wall making him want to turn and shout at her to stop. But they needed a clearly marked path out of the winding, meandering caves. He reached out and pressed the back of his right hand on the cool wall but felt no vibration of anyone else walking down this particular tunnel. Slocum dragged his hand along the rock a few inches without finding any moisture at all. He guessed this dryness was the reason no animals came into the cave. And in spite of what the Sioux hunter had told him, Slocum believed there was some taboo around these caves.

He reacted swiftly when he heard a small noise ahead. He moved the lantern higher and one-handedly pointed his rifle down the tunnel.

"Come on out!" Slocum shouted, trying to flush whoever had kicked the small, betraying stone.

"There is no one there," Anastasia said, peering past him.

"Can you see in the dark?" he said, irritated.

"Better than you. You forget. In St. Petersburg, the win-

ters are not only cold, but the nights are very long. I spend
more time in the dark than you."

Slocum had to laugh at this, breaking the tension. Anastasia frowned and looked up at him.

"I do not understand. Did I say something funny?"

"Maybe not," Slocum said, pushing her request aside.
He cocked his head to one side and listened hard. Her
eyes might be better in the dark than his. Slocum wasn't
too sure about that, but he wasn't going to argue with
Anastasia over it. But he was certain his hearing was more
acute. He lived by the crush of a leaf and the snap of a
twig in the forest.

Moving against the wind gusting from deeper in the
earth, he sniffed hard and listened harder. Without a word,
he handed the lantern to Anastasia and motioned for her
to stay put. Then he advanced slowly, both hands steady-
ing the rifle. When he came to a small crossing tunnel,
he spun as he saw movement a dozen yards down the
straight corridor.

"Freeze!" Slocum yelled. He fired when the dim shape
bolted and ran like a scared rabbit. His slug whined off a
wall and ricocheted past the fleeing man. Slocum fired
again, taking more time to aim, but the shadowy shape
vanished like fog in the morning sun.

He took out after his quarry, quickly finding the small
crevice where the man had taken cover. A scrap of dark
cloth clung to a jagged tip of rock. He started to follow
when he heard Anastasia running up behind him. The
scratch of chalk against rock accompanied the woman.
She continued to mark their path out of the cave.

"Be careful when you fire, John," she warned.

"I know," Slocum said. "But my target wasn't either of
your Cossacks."

She nodded, then held up the lantern and cautiously
looked into the crevice where the man had fled.

"We go into this?"

Slocum hesitated, as he considered. The passage was too tight for him to walk without turning to one side to accommodate his broad shoulders. Slocum knew a trap when he saw it.

"No," he said. "I want whoever it was rooting around in the tunnels, but we're not going to get him by playing his game." Slocum ducked to let some of the light from Anastasia's lantern slip off into the darkness. The light was swallowed by the black maw less than ten feet away.

"There has been someone along this tunnel recently," Anastasia said, backing into the main branch. "Your mysterious man might have come this way, then fled to a hiding spot."

"That poses the question of what he was doing when he came across us," Slocum said. He set off down the tunnel, knowing he left the shadowy man behind them, but he lengthened his stride to hurry them along.

Within minutes they came to a large cavern. Slocum stopped so fast that Anastasia bumped into him.

"What is it?" she asked. "Have you found something?"

"Just looking at the odd roof," Slocum said. The box-like pattern appeared to be carved from lace, but he tapped it with the muzzle of his rifle and found only solid rock. The color varied from white to a pinkish as it stretched into the vaulted dome. On the floor grew dozens of small lumps of rock, less colorful but even more solid.

"There, John. See it?"

Slocum had already spotted the pile of blankets. He stepped aside, checked their back trail, then poked through the blankets. A few personal items tumbled from the pile but other than a straight razor and a knife with a broken blade, he found no weapons.

"A fire was built here," Anastasia said, scuffing her boot across a sooty patch in a nearby hollow. "I don't see anything to show this is more than a temporary camp."

"One man," Slocum said. The skinny ghost he had run

across several times fit the bill. Ned Bartlett would be with his wife. Petersen and Coltrane were dead, as was Yuri Balushkin. "Do you know how many men were with Balushkin?"

"No," she said, "but this is not Russian gear."

"Might have been bought locally," Slocum said.

"There is no tea, no vodka, nothing to show a real Russian camped here."

Slocum prowled around the huge room and found four other small tunnels leading away, in addition to the one they had followed here.

"I don't see that we've gained anything," Slocum said. "No scepter, no Bartletts, nothing." He examined each of the tunnels leading away from the room and found evidence all had been used recently. Slocum wished he had found someone in Goldust or the Sioux camp who knew these caves. Hunting the endless miles of tunnels was futile.

"You are not backing out, John," Anastasia said firmly. "I have made a sacred pledge to my czar. I will not return to the Winter Palace until I have the symbol of my ruler's power with me."

"Bartlett's in here somewhere," Slocum said, "but I don't know how to find him. Building a fire and trying to smoke him out is pointless with the wind blowing all the time. There are too many ways in and out of the caves, anyway. If we flushed Bartlett, he might not have the scepter with him."

"And there are many cave openings," Anastasia finished. "I never thought it would be easy retrieving the scepter." She made a slow circuit of the room, studying the same openings Slocum had. Anastasia stopped in front of one, pushed back a vagrant strand of her black hair and pointed. "This one. We go this way."

"Why?"

The Russian duchess shot him a fierce look and started

down the tunnel, bending low to get into the narrow space before it widened so she could stand upright. Slocum cursed under his breath. Anastasia had the lantern, and he had no choice but to follow her. The more he prowled around underground, the less hope he had that they would find anything worthwhile.

In spite of his growing pessimism, Slocum saw no other way of finding the Bartletts or Czar Alexander's precious gold scepter. They had to stay on enemy land and fight it out here.

"Fight it out," he scoffed. "First, we have to find someone to fight!"

"Quiet! Ahead, John," the woman said sharply. "I see something. A light." Her voice dropped to a husky whisper. "Who is it?"

Slocum worried that it was the mysterious stranger who seemed more ghostlike than human he had encountered earlier. But as the lantern ahead bobbed and danced, Slocum saw Ned Bartlett on his knees scratching at the rock floor.

"There're two of them," Slocum said. The words were hardly out of his mouth when Elizabeth Bartlett stepped into plain view, holding the lantern for her husband. Ned Bartlett jumped as if he had been stuck with a pin and went for a pistol in his belt.

"Kill him!" screeched Elizabeth. "Shoot!"

Slocum reacted a fraction of a second before Ned Bartlett. The rifle bullet missed Bartlett's head by inches, causing the man to tumble backward and fire wildly at the ceiling. Bullets ricocheted off the rock and brought down a cascade of dust that obscured Slocum's view.

"Hold on!" Slocum called.

"Kill him. It's Slocum and that Russian bitch!"

Slocum pushed Anastasia behind him as Bartlett continued to shoot blindly. The slugs tore past them, but one blasted off enough rock near Slocum's face to fill his eyes with dust. Involuntarily, he bent forward and rubbed at his eyes. Behind, he heard Anastasia catch her breath. Then he was deafened by the duchess firing both her six-shooters at the same time. She produced a hail of bullets that forced Bartlett and his wife back.

By the time Slocum got his vision back, the Bartletts had hightailed it deeper into the caves.

"What were they doing, John?" asked Anastasia. "Other than trying to kill us?"

He advanced cautiously, choking on the rock dust still drifting down from the ceiling. The lantern caught the particles and turned the entire room into a fog-like atmosphere.

"I don't know what they were doing," Anastasia said, dropping to her knees and brushing away the dust from the rock where Bartlett had been working so diligently. "There are scratches here."

"A map? Maybe Yuri hid the scepter and scratched a map onto a rock." That sounded crazy to him but nothing about the Russians—or the Bartletts or any of the others killing each other—made a whit of sense to him. No scepter was worth this kind of trouble, even if it was pure gold.

Then he realized why he was hidden away underground hunting for the Bartletts. He wanted to bring Matt Scoggins's killer to justice. For no reason other than duty, honor, friendship. He would feel some small vindication for his good friend's death, but he wouldn't profit from it and Scoggins would still be dead.

Somehow, finding Scoggins's killer still struck Slocum as the better reason to be risking his own life.

"It might be a map, but it is nothing I can decipher. You look, John."

Slocum knelt, trying to keep alert to any attack the Bartletts might launch against him. Anastasia held the lan-

tern close to the rock to allow him to study it. He shook
his head and looked up at her.

"I can't make head nor tail of it. Let's get Bartlett to
tell us why he thought it was so all-fired important."

Choking, squinting to keep his eyes as clear of rock
dust as possible, Slocum got to the far end of the gallery.
Barely had he stepped from the cloud of dust than Bartlett
opened fire on him.

Slocum returned fire, his rifle knocking away huge
hunks of rock around the opening where Bartlett had
taken cover. By the time his magazine came up empty,
he had driven Bartlett deeper into the caves.

"Let's go after them, but be careful," Slocum said. Re-
luctantly, he dropped his rifle and drew his Colt Navy.
Chancing a quick glance around the edge of the tunnel,
all he saw was darkness beyond. Anastasia held up the
lantern, but the tunnel twisted within a few yards, blocking any view of their quarry. The light showed him nothing he hadn't already figured out by listening hard.

Slocum walked on cat's feet to the bend and poked his
head around. Nothing. Anastasia thrust out the lantern
enough to show him a straight, longer stretch of tunnel
that went into a smaller chamber than the one they had
just left.

"I don't see them," Slocum said.

"They are cowards. They have run to find a hiding
place farther into the cave," Anastasia said with some contempt.

Slocum wasn't so sure. Elizabeth Bartlett struck him as
cagey and willing to work any angle she could find to get
her way. She had her sights set on the scepter, and nothing
was going to stop her. Slocum took a step into the chamber and looked around. His eyes widened at the box patterns on the ceiling. Then he reeled backward when an
explosion went off, almost in his face.

He crashed into Anastasia, knocking her into the tunnel they had just traversed.

"What's going on?" demanded Anastasia. A deep rumble drowned out her words as the chamber ceiling collapsed, blocking their path forward.

"Get back," Slocum said, scrambling to get to his feet. He helped Anastasia but she was slow, too slow. He heard a sound like rotten wood creaking, then the tunnel roof ahead collapsed, plunging them into total darkness as the gust of wind and torrent of dust snuffed out the lantern's candle.

Slocum caught up Anastasia in his arms and held her tightly until the rumblings died down. He whispered in her ear, "Breath through your sleeve. It'll block out the dust."

"Da," she said. Anastasia said a great deal more, all in Russian he didn't understand, but the tone was readily understandable. She was cursing her black fate for getting trapped like this.

Slocum wasn't sure the Bartletts had anything to do with the ceiling collapsing on them. It hardly mattered at the moment since they were boxed into a length of tunnel he estimated to be barely ten feet long.

"Quit pacing, John," Anastasia said irritably.

"I'm trying to figure out how much space we have," he said. There was more to it than this. He had heard how miners trapped in cave-ins suffocated. The ever-present wind blowing through these caves was gone now—and so was any other source of fresh air.

"Get a match and light the lantern," Anastasia said. "I do not like it in the dark."

"That'll use our air faster," Slocum said. He saw no reason to sugarcoat their dilemma.

"What will we use the air for, if not to burn our candle?" she asked. Slocum heard rocks being tossed back in his direction. One struck his leg, showing Anastasia was digging like a hound to clear the rockfall leading back into the larger chamber where they had found the Bartletts.

Slocum didn't have a quick answer for the woman's question. He was no expert, but he knew they couldn't last very long in such a small coffin-like stretch of tunnel. Hours? Possibly. Minutes? Definitely.

"Let me dig, too," Slocum said, pressing close to the duchess. For what seemed an eternity they worked at moving the rock, then sat down to rest. Sweat ran down his face in spite of the coolness in the cave.

"Have we gotten any closer to getting out?" asked Anastasia. "Light a match. We need to see if we have made any progress."

Slocum got out his tin of lucifers, glad that he had bought new ones in Goldust. He struck one on a rock and held up the flaring match. The sulfur smell filled his nostrils and made him cough, but he saw how little they had done to get past the plug of rock.

The match died along with his hope for getting out of this rocky prison. Slocum sat with his back against the barrier and thought hard. Nothing came to him. They could keep digging until their fingers were bloody and still not escape. But what other course of action was there for them?

"John?" Anastasia's soft voice was followed by a fleeting touch as she reached out to touch his cheek. She stroked along it. "We are not going to get free, are we?"

"Doesn't much look like it," Slocum said. He pressed Anastasia's fingers into his flesh, turned slightly and kissed the dirty fingertips. She moved closer.

"I do not wish to give up, John, but I will not die without knowing the feel of your body one more time."

The kiss was clumsy, their mouths meeting in the darkness. But once Slocum had the range, he had no more problems. He kissed Anastasia hard, all his pent-up frustrations turning into passion for the beautiful Russian duchess. His hands stroked over her long, dark hair and worked down her shoulders, her arms and around to cup her large breasts. He squeezed gently, firmly and brought gasps of sharp desire to the woman's lips.

"In this darkness, making love becomes so different," Anastasia said.

"Not so different," Slocum said. "I can still feel your heart beating." He slid his hand under her blouse and up across bare skin to trap her left nipple between thumb and forefinger. He tweaked the pulsing pebble of flesh and caused her to shove her chest forward to crush her breast into his palm.

He obliged by kneading the entire mound of satiny flesh and then moving to the other. Anastasia's breath came faster and faster. She moved away a little and stripped off her blouse so she was naked to the waist. Slocum knew, not because he could see her beauty but because he had to feel it. Inch after inch of sleek skin flowed under his questing hands.

"Oh, yes, John. You do that so well."

Slocum grunted as she returned the favor. Her dancing fingers stripped away his gun belt and worked feverishly on the buttons holding his jeans. He wiggled around and let her strip his pants down enough to expose his crotch. Slocum sucked in his breath as Anastasia's fingers clamped firmly around his erect organ.

She held it securely as she homed in on the very tip. Her rough, wet tongue darted across the end and sent tremors of desire lancing into Slocum's loins. When her tongue snaked out and roved the underside, Slocum found himself robbed of speech. All he could do was lean back and let her work on him.

She took the hairy bag she found by sense of feel alone and gently squeezed it as she moved her lips up and down the trembling length of his manhood. Then Anastasia pulled away.

"I am gasping for breath. Is the air going bad?"

"Not yet," Slocum said. "We're doing it to each other." He slid his hands down her sleek flanks and went a bit lower, finding her pertly curved rump. Slocum lifted and guided the duchess to him, her legs parting as she straddled his waist.

He reached down under her skirts and pushed the frilly undergarment out of the way. Heat boiled from her interior, giving him a target to aim at. She shifted around over him as he steered her down. When the knobbed end of his shaft touched her nether lips, Anastasia paused.

"So good. I can forget about . . . everything else."

"No more talking," Slocum ordered. He bent forward and sucked her left nipple into his mouth to give it a tongue-lashing. Then he moved to the other jug and had his way there.

The effect on Anastasia was obvious. She had been tense. As his lips and tongue and teeth raked across her delicate, sensitive nipples, she sank down. As she did, he plunged deep into her moist, yearning interior.

"This is divine, John. What I need. What *we* need."

He twisted around under her, stirring his meaty shaft in her tight passage. Then she lifted a little, leaving him out in the cold. But not for long. Anastasia plummeted back down, taking him entirely into her female sheath and gripping hard with her inner muscles.

As they strove together, their desires rose. Slocum lifted from the rocky pile where he sat and shoved himself harder and harder into the woman's eagerly awaiting cavity. He kissed her breasts and stroked her bare back, tracing over every bone in her spine. Slocum tried hard to keep from spilling his seed too soon.

But the heat mounted uncontrollably along his steely piston and spread throughout his loins. He body blazed with need, and when Anastasia cried out her release, he was unable to hold back any longer. He rammed up into her, trying to split her apart. She dropped down hard and shuddered through a second orgasm.

This was more than Slocum could withstand. He felt the fiery tide rising within him blast forth uncontrollably. They continued to struggle and strive together until both were exhausted from their efforts. Anastasia lay forward, her breasts crushing into Slocum's chest. Their crotches pressed together and their legs rubbed.

But all Slocum felt now was the woman's soft, hot breath gasping out against his cheek. A breath that would soon be extinguished, along with all their air.

17

Slocum felt Anastasia stir gently in his arms. She had fallen asleep after their amorous activity, but he had stayed awake. Slocum worried that he was missing some way to escape their trap, but the more he worried on the notion like a hound dog with a bone, the more he realized they had done all they could. Moving the tons of rock that had collapsed was a chore a dozen miners could not do easily in weeks, even working with blasting powder, picks and a method to get the rock hauled away from the tunnel before shoring it up.

Slocum's hands moved restlessly over Anastasia's warm, bare skin, feeling the silky smoothness and the way it rippled a little from the cool air in the tunnel. She had pulled on her blouse but had not buttoned it, leaving it gaping open in the front.

He closed his eyes, went over every possible way to escape and then heaved a deep sigh of resignation. They had done their best and would end their time on earth with the pleasurable memories of each other's body.

Slocum opened his eyes to the darkness and blinked, thinking he was seeing ghosts. He reached up and rubbed his eyes, getting the last of the dust from his vision. He stood up so fast that Anastasia banged against the rock and came awake with a startled cry.

"What is wrong, John?" she asked. "I was having a dream. I thought we were—oh."

"Look at the ceiling. Do you see what I do?"

"I—light! I see light. Not much, John, but there is light!"

"And air. We're not going to suffocate in here. I thought I felt a cool breeze against my hands, and I did." Slocum climbed onto a rock, stretched as far as he dared without losing his balance, pressed his face against the ceiling and sniffed hard. Fresh, cold air.

Slocum slid his fingers into the crevice and strained hard, trying to part the rock. He felt a sharp pain in his side where the bullet crease opened again. Slocum ignored the pain and kept up the pressure when he felt the rock begin to crumble. He fell back heavily into Anastasia's arms when the rock gave way suddenly and came plunging down on top of him. Sputtering and thrashing, he got up.

Anastasia pushed him aside and got to her feet. A single ray of light shone through the chimney opening onto the surface and outlined her perfectly, as if she stood center stage in a spotlight. He caught his breath, seeing what he had missed of her beauty during their unlit lovemaking. Her blouse hung open, exposing her creamy breasts, and her pale face was upturned and exultant.

"Air, John! It never felt better." She let out a cry of joy as she spun about.

Slocum got to his feet and studied the chimney that had opened. By prying open the bottom of the shaft, he had given them a way to escape. The chimney was narrow but big enough even for Slocum to climb.

"Go on," he told Anastasia. "You first. I'll follow."

Anastasia laughed in delight. "You men. You just want to look up my skirt!" She scrambled up without another word, pressing her back against one side of the rock shaft and her feet against the other. Inching up, she soon blotted out the light from above. Then she vanished entirely.

"Anastasia!" Slocum called.

"I am fine, John. It is cold up here, but I am free!" She stopped speaking and disappeared from the top of the chimney.

Slocum gathered their gear, tied the lantern to his belt and made sure his six-shooter was secured in its holster, then started the climb. For him the way was a tighter fit but within ten minutes he flopped into a snowbank already marked with Anastasia's boot prints. He looked around for her, but the woman was nowhere to be seen.

Slocum got to his feet and brushed himself off, then drew his six-gun against trouble. There was no reason for Anastasia to disappear so quickly.

"Anastasia! Where'd you go?"

He spun in a full circle, worrying that she had come to grief in such a hurry. Then he settled down, looked at the tracks the woman had left in the snow and started after them. He saw paw prints of a small coyote and the larger track of a full-grown rabbit—the coyote's prey—but no human spoor other than the woman's trail.

"Anastasia!" he called again, as he trudged up a low hill almost fifty yards from where the vent had exited the caves. Slocum went into a crouch, his six-gun ready for action when he caught sudden movement out of the corner of his eye. He relaxed when he saw the dark-haired woman, grinning ear to ear.

"John, look what I have found!"

"Why'd you go off like that?" he demanded.

"I saw vapor rising. I thought something was afire and came to investigate. See?" Anastasia pointed to a large hole in the ground where steam spewed forth. Slocum tentatively moved his hand into the cloud of vapor erupting from below. It was as cool as the wind blowing from the cave mouth but must have picked up a considerable amount of water along the way to form such a fog.

"This leads back down into the caves," Anastasia said excitedly. "See how we can go down? There is almost a ladder. Not like the chimney we climbed out of before."

"You want to go back into the caves?" Slocum hardly believed his ears. "Why don't we hunt for your two servants? We can use them to watch our backs."

"They are still underground, hunting for the scepter. Where I should be." Anastasia dusted off her hands and dropped to sit on the edge of the vent. She recoiled as her face passed through the steam. "Wet," she said. "There must be ledges below holding snow. The wind from below melts the snow, brings up the water and turns it into fog when it contacts the cold outer air."

"If you say so." Slocum listened to the duchess with half an ear. He had already figured this out for himself. He had other matters to worry over. There could be no doubt Anastasia felt honor bound to recover her ruler's scepter, but Slocum hesitated. He didn't usually feel any uneasiness at being in mine shafts, but he had spent too much time below. Having the ceiling collapse on him had soured him on doing any more cave exploring.

"You will not accompany me?" she asked. Anastasia's dark eyes fixed on him. "I do not blame you," she said, "but I thought you would want to find who set off the explosion. Dynamite? Or was it only black powder?"

"What're you talking about?" Slocum asked.

"The cave-in. It was not natural. There had to be an explosion to bring down the ceiling."

"I didn't hear any explosion."

"I did. But you may stay here, if that is your wish. Hand me the lantern and a few of your friction matches. I will need the light below."

"I can't let you go," Slocum said, studying Anastasia closely. He was a damned good poker player and knew how to tell if someone lied to him. If Anastasia was spinning a wild tale about dynamite, she didn't show it in either her expression or the set to her shapely body.

"You cannot stop me, John," she said firmly.

"You heard an explosion?"

Anastasia smiled and shrugged. "You will believe what you will. Think back yourself."

Slocum did for a moment. He had been shooting, listening to Elizabeth shout at her husband, and had been too occupied to hear any detonation. If anything, his ears had rung with the sound of too much gunfire. But he remembered a curious smell afterward, the distinctive smell of dynamite after it had been detonated.

"I'll go first. I have the lantern lashed down already." He sat beside her, frowned at how stupid he could be, then slid into the steamy rock vent.

Slocum found a ledge a few feet lower, covered in melting snow as Anastasia had predicted. Below that were other ledges, as if nature had provided a ladder back into the caverns. Before he knew it, Slocum dangled from the last rocky outcropping, his feet swinging freely in the air. He took a deep breath and then let loose, falling into darkness.

Slocum plunged downward less than eight feet before crashing into the cave floor. He hit with bent knees and rolled, banging up the lantern. He came to his feet, listened intently for any hint that anyone else was nearby, then lit the lantern and held it aloft.

Twenty feet away at the far end of the cavern he saw a rockfall. Before he could examine it to see if this led to the tunnel where he and Anastasia had been trapped, he looked up to see the woman's boots appear. He put down the lantern in time to catch her with both arms as she dropped. He held her in his arms for a moment, remembering the time they had shared in the coffin-like tunnel not so long before. She smiled, kissed him and lightly dropped.

"We can now begin the hunt for the scepter," she said happily.

"Wait," he said when she started away from the rock-fall. "I want to be sure I have my bearings."

"Beyond that is where we were imprisoned," Anastasia said, pointing to the pile of rocks. "My sense of direction is quite good, even underground."

Slocum ignored her eagerness to tear off in the opposite direction. He wasn't sure what drew him to the rocks, but he was glad he had taken the time to examine them. Poking out from under the tumbled-down pile was a pair of boots.

He exchanged a quick glance with Anastasia, then began the chore of moving the rocks off the body. The boots were scuffed and old, convincing him they didn't belong to either of Anastasia's Cossacks. Within minutes, he had tossed aside enough rock to expose Ned Bartlett's blood-ied, crushed face.

"He died too quickly," Anastasia said without remorse.

"You reckon he threw the dynamite and got trapped?" Slocum asked. He kept moving the rock until the man's body was fully exposed. Patting down the pockets failed to reveal even a package of lucifers. "You see where his lantern is?"

"No," Anastasia said. "He looks as if he ran from the other chamber, the one where the dynamite brought down the roof, and did not escape in time."

"Escape," Slocum said, turning the word over and over. "Like he saw his wife throw the dynamite from here and couldn't get out of the chamber fast enough."

"She killed him, too?"

Slocum held their lantern high and looked around until he found a burnt match a few feet away. He pictured Elizabeth Bartlett holding a stick of dynamite, lighting the fuse, then going to the mouth of the cavern and throwing the dynamite so it would kill not only her husband but also Slocum and Anastasia in the tunnel beyond.

"Here," Anastasia said. "This is a blasting cap." She held up the crushed metal tube.

"Toss it away. Those things are powerful enough to blow off your hand. Somebody—Elizabeth—tried to crimp it and didn't make it the first time. She used a second cap, got the fuse attached to the stick of dynamite and then lit it." He searched the area where Elizabeth had so cold-bloodedly worked to kill her husband, looking for any clue to the woman's whereabouts in the caves. Slocum looked up at Anastasia, the same thought occurring to them both at the same time.

"She knows where the scepter is," Anastasia said.

Slocum went back to Bartlett's squashed body and knelt, rolling the man over.

"This looks familiar," he said grimly. He pointed to a bullet hole in the center of Bartlett's back. "She shot him, then threw the dynamite to bury him—and us."

"It is time we found this bitch and stopped her," Anastasia said. "She has killed enough, and she has the czar's scepter."

Slocum couldn't have agreed more with the duchess's sentiments. He checked to be certain his Colt Navy was fully loaded and ready for action, then set out after Anastasia into the maze of caves leading away from Ned Bartlett.

18

"The light will warn her we're coming," Slocum said. "She'll go to ground and hide until we're past."

Anastasia Zharkov looked around the large cavern they had entered, turning slowly as she studied every nook and cranny in the walls for sign of Elizabeth Bartlett. The duchess did not respond to Slocum's concern about trapping the other woman as she climbed onto a large rock to give her a better view.

Slocum handed her the lantern and went to hunt for Elizabeth on his own, wary of an attack. They had found traces of the woman's passage that disquieted him. Elizabeth had dropped four more blasting caps and a length of black miner's fuse. He had no idea if she also had a few sticks of dynamite with her. If so, she could bring down the vaulted ceiling of this cavern without much effort.

Slocum shuddered at the idea of being buried alive again. The first time had been pleasant enough, as it turned out. There had been a certain determination and frantic need for satisfaction in the lovemaking with Anastasia since they had both thought they were doomed and this would be their last chance at affirming their life and passion. But now that they were free again, Slocum felt a hesitation about what Elizabeth Bartlett might do to them.

He could face any man with a six-shooter. In his day he had fought off gangs of outlaws—and lawmen. Being buried was something that would happen to him some day, as it had already happened with Matt Scoggins, but to be buried alive sent shivers up and down his spine.

"There," Anastasia said, pointing to her left. "I see a small hole where she went."

"Is she following a map or just looking for the scepter by searching every room she comes to?" asked Slocum. If Elizabeth was tearing through the maze of caves, they weren't as likely to find her. If the murderous woman knew where the scepter had been hidden, they might blunder on her as she retrieved it.

"Quiet, John." Anastasia put her finger to her lips.

Slocum heard the small sounds, like a trapped animal trying to escape a trap on its leg. He drew his six-gun and quietly went to the small hole, hardly large enough for him to wiggle through. Slocum fought down a moment of fear. He didn't know where this led or what he would find, but he knew it was a tight fit. Like a coffin. In the dark.

"I will go first, John," Anastasia said.

"No!"

"I am smaller. I will not become caught in this hole."

"Elizabeth had dynamite. She might be waiting to toss a stick into the tunnel," he warned.

Anastasia shrugged it off. "This is for my czar."

The sounds that had echoed along the tunnel disappeared as they stood arguing. Slocum and Anastasia exchanged a look, his green eyes boring into her dark ones. He took the lantern from her resisting fingers, then dropped to his knees and pushed the lamp ahead of him as he squirmed into the hole.

The light almost blinded Slocum as he shoved it at arm's length ahead of him. His toes caught at the smooth rock floor, but he managed to make his way forward. He heaved a sigh of relief when the lantern showed another room, bigger than the one he had left.

Slocum scrambled to his feet, six-shooter ready for action. He went into a gunfighter's crouch and pointed his weapon directly at sounds across the rocky room. He caught a glimpse of a figure cloaked in blackness diving down behind a rounded rock.

"Come out with your hands up!" Slocum called. His words rang through the room. He glanced down to see Anastasia working her way out of the hole to stand beside him.

"Who is it? The Bartlett bitch?"

Slocum cautioned her to silence. He indicated that she should circle left while he went right to trap their quarry between them. Slocum moved fast, wanting to keep the upper hand.

He got to the point where he had seen movement in time to see a pair of battered boots vanishing into a hole so small he could never hope to follow. Slocum shoved his six-shooter into its holster and dived, grabbing the boots with both hands. He avoided two feeble kicks and then dug in and started pulling hard, like he was reeling in a fish.

When the man popped out of the hole, he tried to get away, only to find himself staring into the twin bores of Anastasia's pistols.

"Where is the scepter?" she said coldly. Then she frowned. "Who the hell are you?"

"I think I've caught me a sneak thief," Slocum said, staring at the gaunt, poorly dressed man sitting on the rocky floor, looking more frightened by the instant.

"No, not me, I'm not a thief!"

"You rummaged through my saddlebags," Slocum said.

He was positive this was the owlhoot who had tried to rob him after he had weathered the blizzard on his way to Goldust. He had seen him a few more times during his hunt through the caves, every time thinking he was more of a skeletal ghost than a human being.

The man was pale like a cave-dwelling animal and emaciated to the point of starvation. His black broadcloth coat was a couple of sizes too big and hung in tatters, giving him a flapping bat aspect when he moved around. Muddy brown eyes peered up at Slocum from the bottom of deep pits. Try as he might, Slocum couldn't read what went on in those eyes. He expected more animal than human to be present there, but even this was masked.

"I don't know you, but I seen you 'round. You and the rest of them've been comin' into my caves."

"You live here?" asked Anastasia. The eagerness in her voice told Slocum she thought she had found her guide to the czar's scepter. Slocum had to admit she might be right. He had hunted Goldust for someone who knew the labyrinth and had failed. Not even the Sioux had explored this vast underground kingdom. This miserable example of humanity might just be what Slocum had sought futilely.

"All mine," the pale man said with some pride. "Nobody else comes 'round. Not till lately. I tried to drive 'em off, but they kept on botherin' me."

"The woman was the worst, wasn't she?" asked Slocum. He didn't have to describe Elizabeth to get a response.

"She killed that fellow. The big one. The one dressed like *her* friends." The man pointed at Anastasia.

"Balushkin?" Slocum directed the question to Anastasia, who only shook her head angrily. She cared nothing about Yuri Balushkin's death. What mattered was the czar's scepter.

"Where did the man she killed put the gold scepter?"

The man blinked, opened his mouth but no words came out. He looked up at Slocum with immense pleading in his gaze. Slocum reckoned the man didn't cotton much to women. Maybe they scared him or perhaps he had been a hermit so long he didn't like being questioned directly.

"The other woman's got dynamite," Slocum said. "She'll blow up this entire place if you don't help me stop her."

"Dynamite, yes, yes," the man said almost pathetically. "Dangerous here. The roof can fall on me."

"My name's Slocum. What's yours?"

"Ed. They call me Ed."

"Ed," Slocum said seriously, "I need your help to stop her. You don't want what she has, do you?"

"The gold pipe?" Ed answered.

Slocum shot Anastasia a quick look to keep her quiet. "What happened to it?"

"The big man, the one dressed like her," Ed said, looking at Anastasia, "hid the pipe in the cave and made a map. The woman killed him, but I fooled her. I took the map. He never knew I took his map. He was dead, anyway."

"You have the map?" Anastasia couldn't restrain herself. She grabbed Ed by his thin shoulders and shook. Slocum fancied he could hear bones rattling.

"No, he stole it! He stole it from my house!"

"Who?" shouted Anastasia, shaking him harder. Slocum grabbed her arm and pulled the duchess away. "Tell me what happened to the map!"

"This is real important, Ed," Slocum said. "Tell me what happened." He felt the same urgency and frustration that Anastasia did, but he saw that Ed was a little on the simple side.

"I put it with my gear, but the other man, the one she blew up with the dynamite, he stole it from me. He took some of my food, too And a bunch of candles."

"Ned Bartlett," Slocum said. "That was the man's name. So you're telling me the other woman took the map and then blew him up?"

Ed's head bobbed up and down like it was on a spring.

"No, it cannot be," moaned Anastasia. "We'll never find Elizabeth or the scepter now!"

Slocum studied Ed carefully and saw the way he averted his mud-colored eyes. It was too bad Ed didn't play poker. Slocum would have cleaned him out in a few hands.

"Where is the map, Ed?"

"She has it. The one you're callin' Elizabeth."

"She has the map, but you know something about that map, don't you?"

"You saw the map," Anastasia said anxiously. "You memorized it, didn't you? Yes! I see it in your face!" She started to shake Ed again, but Slocum stepped between the irate duchess and the scarecrow of a man.

"Can you lead us to the spot marked on the map, Ed? Do you know what's hidden there?"

"The pipe. The gold pipe, I reckon."

"Go on, show us how to get there," Slocum said.

"You won't hurt me?" Ed cringed, not from Slocum but from Anastasia.

"We'll give you whatever you want," Anastasia assured him.

"Want to be left alone. My caves. Everyone should stay away."

"Food," Slocum promised. "We'll see that you get food, if you can take us to the gold pipe."

Ed looked furtive, then nodded. "I can do that. But you gotta leave me alone."

"No one will disturb you," said Anastasia.

Slocum took her aside and said quietly, "He's afraid of you. Let me talk to him. If he takes it into his head to lose us in the cave and just vanishes, we won't find him or the scepter."

"He lives in these caves?" Anastasia asked. She sounded amazed at such a hermit.

"Why not? The Sioux avoid the place like it was the mouth to hell, no animals come into the caves because there's no water, and I suspect most white men riding through never even notice the openings, in spite of the constant wind blowing out. I wouldn't have, except I blundered into the hot air."

"The scepter, John. I know it is close. I must get it!"

"All right," Slocum said. He held her back to keep the anxious Russian duchess from spooking Ed. She stayed behind him with great reluctance. Slocum turned to Ed and said, "Where do we go to find the gold pipe?"

Ed swallowed hard, his prominent Adam's apple bobbing. He pointed, then got to his feet and started for a dark corner of the giant vaulted room. A small tunnel Slocum had missed entirely led away. He made certain a fresh candle burned in his lantern, then set off after the reluctant Ed. The tunnel was narrow and gave Slocum a few pangs, then he stopped worrying about getting buried alive and started examining the strange mineral structures along the walls. They came in delicate, lacy patterns and bold colored ones.

Before he knew it, Ed turned and thrust out a bony finger that stabbed into Slocum's chest.

"Ahead. That's where the map showed it to be. I call it the Dog Room." Ed smiled shyly. "I never had a dog. This one's not real. It's made outta rock, but it looks real stickin' up smack-dab in the middle. If you don't try to get it to do no tricks, I mean. But it don't eat or mess none. Sometimes I fancy I can hear 'im barkin', though. I like it when that happens."

Slocum silenced Anastasia's annoyed outburst. He handed her the lantern to keep her occupied while he

pushed Ed in the direction of the tunnel mouth opening
into yet another vast cavern.

"See?" Ed pointed to a silhouette cast on the far wall
by their lantern light. "A dog. I never named 'im."

Slocum nodded. The shadow did look like a big dog,
more than the rock itself did. He hurried to the tower of
rock and looked around the base. "Is the pipe near the
dog?" Slocum asked Ed. The man looked flustered and
scared out of his wits. Ed wiped his lips on his sleeve and
looked like he wanted to turn and bolt.

"There's nothing but solid rock here," Slocum said,
looking around. "No one's dug into this, not unless they
blasted with dynamite. And I don't see any evidence that's
happened."

"This's where the X was on the map. Honest," Ed said.
He backed up and pressed hard into another rock spire.

"I see nothing," Anastasia said, circling the stone base
in the opposite direction. "He lies!"

"No, no, not lyin'," Ed said, cringing.

"What's that?" Slocum clamped his hand over Ed's
mouth to shut him up. "Close the lantern shutter," he ordered Anastasia. She hurriedly obeyed, shutting the small
door until only a sliver of pale yellow light leaked out.
The duchess put the lantern on the floor and drew her
brace of pistols.

Someone was singing off-key at the other end of the
cavern. Slocum edged around the rock dog and saw the
bobbing of a miner's candle coming in from the far side
of the room.

"Her!" Ed said around Slocum's muffling hand. "The
one with the dynamite!"

Anastasia was already gone, cutting across the room in
the direction of the far wall to circle and come up on
Elizabeth Bartlett from the side. Slocum kicked out and
closed the door entirely on the lantern, snuffing out the
candle. Plunged into darkness, Slocum was better able to

see the miner's candle that Elizabeth carried.

"Where can we hide?" Slocum whispered to Ed. "Somewhere nearby?"

Ed gobbled like a turkey until Slocum shut him up by shoving the muzzle of his six-shooter into the man's bony ribs. Under this goading, Ed turned and scrambled off amid the small stony forest of spires until he came to a hollow behind a waist-high column. He ducked down, drew up his knees and buried his face between his knees.

Slocum put down his lantern, then turned to watch as Elizabeth came through the room to the spot where he had stood only seconds earlier. The woman pressed a map against the foot of the dog, then swept the candle back and forth a few times.

Slocum couldn't figure what she was doing, but something in the strange ritual told her where to look. Elizabeth dropped the map and set off in the direction Anastasia had gone. Slocum wanted to call out to warn the Russian duchess, but he held his tongue and crept after Elizabeth instead. If lead started flying, Slocum didn't want Anastasia to mistake him for Elizabeth Bartlett, but he had no choice.

Gunshots rang out and sounds of a struggle filled the huge room. Then there was only silence, the terrifying silence of the grave.

19

"Anastasia!" shouted Slocum. He stumbled and almost fell in the darkness. The candle Elizabeth Bartlett had carried no longer provided a guiding beacon. Cursing, he felt his way back to the spot where Ed still crouched and shook in fear. Slocum pulled out a lucifer, struck it on the rock above Ed's head and waited for the hiss and sudden flare to die down, then opened the lantern gate and relit the candle inside. He wasn't going to blunder around in the pitch blackness of the cave hunting for a woman who had proven herself a murderer.

But Slocum feared what he might find in the pale light from the lantern.

"Anastasia!" he called again. No answer. He advanced warily, holding the lantern high and to his left to draw fire should Elizabeth take it into her head to kill him. And why shouldn't she? The woman had already admitted to killing Mikhail and evidence went against her when it came to killing her own husband. She probably did not know how her dynamite blast had also trapped Anastasia and Slocum, nor would it bother her to know.

A bullet whined through the darkness and pinged off the tin lantern, almost taking it from his hand. Slocum had been staring straight ahead into the dark and was blinded by the foot-long orange flame leaping from the bore of a pistol, but he knew where the shooter had to be.

Caution took over. He held back firing. He couldn't see his target clearly and didn't want to make a fatal mistake. Elizabeth Bartlett was out there somewhere—but so was the Russian duchess.

Slocum stayed low and reached a protected area where he could put the lantern atop a rock that would shield him from more bullets. Turning the lantern slowly, shining the light forward, he focused the light on the spot where he had seen the muzzle flash. His heart jumped into his throat at what he saw. He threw caution to the winds and rushed to the fallen woman's side.

"Anastasia," he said, dropping to one knee to see if the woman was still alive. She lay propped against a rock, unconscious. Both her pistols were gone. If Slocum had returned fire at the place where he had seen the muzzle flash, he would have killed Anastasia and not Elizabeth Bartlett. Elizabeth had used the Russian duchess as a shield, hoping Slocum would accidentally shoot the dark-haired woman.

"The bitch," moaned Anastasia. "She . . . she must have known I followed. Hit me." She reached up and touched a bloodied spot on her scalp where Elizabeth had struck her with a rock.

"Don't talk. I'll get her."

"I want her," Anastasia said, strength returning rapidly. "She cannot do this to me! I am a respected member of Czar Alexander the Second's court! I am a duchess!"

"She took your guns," Slocum said, pushing her back down. "I'll get her. She can't light her candle without me spotting her. You stay put." Slocum didn't tell Anastasia how he had almost shot her by accident—because of Elizabeth's diabolical design.

He had to be smarter. And deadlier.

"John, wait," Anastasia said. She grabbed his arm and pulled him back to give him a quick kiss. "The next time, we do not have to make love in the dark. I want to see you in the bright light of day, every inch of you!"

"Stay here," Slocum repeated, then started after Elizabeth, staying low and listening hard for the sounds of the woman's shoes against the rocky floor. Vibration didn't carry in the huge vaulted chamber the way it did down tunnels, so feeling the rock and detecting her movement that way wasn't possible.

Slocum turned a little to his right and fired three times when he heard a pistol cocking. From the lingering flash from his Colt Navy, he saw Elizabeth Bartlett rise up and clutch her right arm. One of Anastasia's heavy six-guns clattered down. Before Slocum could fire again, darkness descended and Elizabeth vanished.

He dropped to his belly and slithered forward like a snake to the spot where he had seen the six-gun fall. Slocum retrieved it, wishing he could tell how many rounds were in its cylinder. He tucked it away in his belt, then continued his hunt for Elizabeth.

"You can't get away," he shouted. Slocum waited for a response so he could go after her. He had no intention of letting her surrender after all she had done. Killing so many men was one thing, trapping Slocum in a rocky prison was something else.

Slocum waited for the woman to betray herself, but Elizabeth Bartlett was too cagey for that. He heard nothing. She might be hiding so she could escape or simply trying to gather her wits. But he doubted either was true. Slocum knew Elizabeth would kill him.

After a few minutes of wondering where she might be, Slocum moved into the darkness. His lantern remained on the rock a dozen yards behind him, but it gave him no advantage.

Worrying that Elizabeth was getting away from him,

Slocum hurried forward. He occasionally picked up a pebble and tossed it to either left or right hoping to draw the woman out, but nothing worked. When Slocum reached the cavern wall, he started to his right. Every step made him worry more that he had missed her.

Slocum had no reason to do it, but he came to a quick decision to retrace his path. He caught sight of the lantern and homed in on it in time to see a shadowy figure slouching along.

"Stop!" Slocum called. When the vague outline turned, Slocum fired. One round went wide and the second time his hammer fell, it clicked on a spent chamber.

Three shots tore through the dark and drove him to cover. Slocum holstered his six-shooter and pulled Anastasia's pistol he had retrieved. He chanced a quick glance around the rock, aimed and fired twice before this six-shooter came up empty. Slocum stuffed it back into his belt and circled to come up on Elizabeth from the side in the faint hope he could tackle her.

Slocum sprinted when he heard sounds of a fierce fight. In the faint light from the lantern he saw Elizabeth and Anastasia locked in a furious wrestling match. Before he could reach them, his boot slid on loose gravel on the floor and he crashed facedown, momentarily stunned. He shook it off and scrambled forward.

"Anastasia?" Slocum saw one shadow figure standing over another. He wasn't sure who had won.

The phantasm turned. Slocum saw a rock in one hand. He froze, not wanting to know what he got himself into.

"John," came the duchess's soft voice. "She attacked me."

Slocum scrambled to his feet and hurried to a point where the light shone past the woman still standing. He saw it was truly Anastasia Zharkov. She dropped a bloody rock with a clatter. Slocum's eyes followed the rock, then swept past to where Elizabeth Bartlett lay sprawled on the dusty cavern floor. She stared upward sightlessly at the curious box formations in the rocky ceiling. Clenched in one fist was Anastasia's stolen pistol.

"It came up empty," Anastasia said. "That saved me. Then I struck her with the rock."

"You saved your life. Mine, too, maybe," Slocum said.

At this Anastasia laughed harshly. "You can take care of yourself too well, John, for me to believe that. There is no need to make me feel better. I *wanted* to kill her for all she had done."

"You succeeded," Slocum said.

For a spell neither said anything, then Anastasia spoke. "Where do we find the scepter?"

Slocum left the body on the cavern floor and wended his way back to where Elizabeth had dropped the map. He wasn't too surprised to find Ed hunched over it, a bony finger tracing out patterns.

"Can you tell us where the gold, uh, pipe is?" Slocum asked.

Ed looked up guiltily.

"We will give you plenty of food. Blankets, too," Anastasia said. "Anything you want."

"You killed her," Ed said, staring at Anastasia with great fear in his eyes. "She was a bad lady."

"Ed," Slocum said, wanting to be done with this.

"If I get you the pipe, will you leave me alone? Don't like folks pokin' 'round my caves. Never have."

"The map," Slocum said, tiring of the flickering light from the lantern and having tons of rock over his head all the time. "What's it tell you?"

"There," Ed said, pointing.

Anastasia and Slocum found a pile of rubble a dozen paces away from Ed's Dog Rock and began digging.

"It was kind of you to see Mikhail laid to rest properly," Anastasia said.

"I didn't know him that well, but I liked him," Slocum said. He looked past the duchess up the hill to the top of Goldust's lonely cemetery. He had suggested taking the Russian's body to Deadwood where Mt. Moriah was better populated, but Anastasia had decided this was a more fitting resting place. Slocum liked the idea that Mikhail was in the grave next to Matt Scoggins. They could swap tall tales for the rest of eternity.

Wind blew down the slope and bit at his cheeks. Slocum turned from the wind to where Anastasia's two Cossacks stood, hands resting on the pistols thrust into their belts. Behind them in the wagon rode a long box about the size of a child's coffin, but inside rested something more precious to Anastasia.

Czar Alexander's scepter.

"I never did find out who killed Scoggins," Slocum said.

"Does it matter so?" asked Anastasia. "The outlaws are dead. One of them must have done it."

"Maybe so," Slocum allowed, "but which one? I can't make him pay any more than he already has, but it'd put my mind at rest."

"Come with me, John," Anastasia said impetuously. "You would love the Winter Palace in St. Petersburg. The czar will welcome you as a conquering hero. You helped get the scepter." In a lower voice, Anastasia added, "My suite of rooms is the finest in the entire palace."

"If you're there, of course they are," Slocum said.

"If we're both in the fine, large bed, we—" She broke off her words when she saw his expression. Anastasia heaved a sigh. Huge gusts of vapor gusted from her nostrils. "You are right. Russia is not the place for you, but it is for me. My czar needs my services. That pig Yuri Balushkin was only one of many who plot Alexander's overthrow. Ever since he freed the serfs from the landowners, Alexander has fought with a small but powerful group of nobles."

"You're used to that kind of fighting," Slocum said. "It's not for me."

"Just for a few months?" Anastasia said with longing.

"No, not even for such a short time. Good-bye, John. Remember me." She stood on tiptoe and quickly kissed him. Then she mounted her powerful stallion and galloped off without a backward glance, the Cossacks riding on either side of the wagon carrying the precious symbol of their czar's power.

Slocum went to Mikhail's fresh grave and stared at the mounded dirt, then at Matt Scoggins's. The earth had compacted, pressing down on the man in the grave. Slocum shuddered. He knew what terrors the grave held after being trapped in the damnable cave-in. And he knew what he had to do next.

The ride out into the countryside took the better part of the day, but Slocum finally found the right cave and dismounted. He pulled a large pack from behind his saddle and dropped it to the ground.

"Ed!" he called. "Here's the food I promised you. And some blankets."

Slocum wondered if he ought to simply ride on, but there was something he had to take care of first. He waited almost fifteen minutes before Ed decided it was safe enough to come out.

"Didn't think you'd come back."

"I keep my word," Slocum said. He watched as Ed rummaged through the food, tossing away cans of vegetables and keeping what he wanted.

Ed looked up, drew the pile he wanted to himself and said, "You keep the rest. Don't want 'em."

"I'll leave them. You might change your mind." Slocum licked his lips, then knew what he had to ask. "Ed?"

"Yeah?"

"Do you know who killed Scoggins?"

"Don't know no Scoggins," Ed said.

"He worked as Duchess Anastasia's guide." Slocum remembered one thing that Anastasia had said that he had ignored before as being improbable. "Do you have a black powder musket, Ed?"

"Need it," Ed said, eyes dropping to the ground. "Don't use it much. Ain't got powder for it, mostly."

"You only use it to drive off unwanted visitors to your caves?" asked Slocum. His hand twitched and started for the ebony handle of his six-shooter, but he held back. Ed looked like a whipped dog.

"You won't tell her, will you?"

"What's that? Tell Anastasia what?" Slocum was confused now.

"She's awful, that foreign devil of a woman. I didn't mean to hit nobody. I was aimin' at them other two, not her."

"Wait, hold your horses," Slocum said, confused. "Tell me exactly what happened. I won't tell Duchess Anastasia. This is between you and me."

"Them men. Petersen and Coltrane. I was shootin' at them, to get them to go away. I ain't so good a shot and missed them by a country mile. The slug flew right on over their heads toward her and that big fella."

"Mikhail?"

"Reckon I heard him called that. But it didn't hit neither her or the big fella. Hit the other guy with them. Damn, but she was mad when he got shot! I didn't mean him no harm. I didn't! I was just tryin' to scare off the other two, Petersen and Coltrane. They was prowlin' about in *my* caves and disturbin' me. They had no right. One of them took a shot at me but missed by a country mile. I lit out then, and so did they 'cuz the duchess was so fumin' mad."

Slocum felt a hollowness inside that wouldn't go away

anytime soon. He had found Matt Scoggins's killer and didn't much like it. The cartridge he had found had been expended at Ed, not Scoggins. He wished he had taken Anastasia's advice and simply ridden away, believing it was one of the pack of owlhoots who had already given their lives trying to steal the czar's gold scepter.

Instead, he had learned the truth, and it didn't make him feel one whit better. Scoggins's death had been a mishap committed by a hermit with an old musket and a poor aim who wanted nothing more than to be left alone.

"You won't tell her? You promised! I don't want her gettin' mad at me!"

"Next time, Ed, be sure of your target before you shoot," Slocum said.

"You leavin'?" The hopefulness in Ed's voice gave Slocum added reason to leave.

"Yeah, Ed, I'm leaving. And don't worry. I won't be back this way."

Slocum rode past the mouth of the cave and felt the devil's breath for what he hoped would be the last time. Mexico would be a far better place to spend the winter, with a bottle of tequila and a warm señorita beside him to while away the days.

That might help him forget Anastasia and what had happened to Matt Scoggins, but Slocum didn't think so.

Watch for

Slocum and the Treasure Chest

290th novel in the exciting SLOCUM series
from Jove

Coming in April!